Now that April's there

Now that April's there

A NOVEL BY

Daisy Neumann

J. B. LIPPINCOTT COMPANY

PHILADELPHIA AND NEW YORK

SECOND IMPRESSION BEFORE PUBLICATION

Printed in the United States of America

Under Government regulations for saving paper during the
war, the size and thickness of this book have been reduced
below the customary peacetime standards. Only the format
has been affected. The text is complete and unabridged.

Oh, to be in England,
Now that April's there,
And whoever wakes in England
Sees, some morning, unaware,
That the lowest boughs and the brush-wood sheaf
Round the elm-tree bole are in tiny leaf,
While the chaffinch sings on the orchard bough
      In England—now!

—ROBERT BROWNING, *Home Thoughts*
From Abroad

For
ELLEN *and* JOHN NICHOLAS

The author acknowledges with thanks the permission of the editors of THE NEW YORKER to reprint the first chapter of this novel, which appeared in their pages in a slightly different version, as a short story.

Foreword

Wincy and Angus Turner never came to the United States. They never lived in Oxford, England. In fact, they never existed at all.

A number of boys and girls did come from Oxford to the United States under circumstances similar to those described in this book and established themselves so firmly in the affections of their foster-families that their subsequent departure caused intense sorrow. Should one of these fancy that Angus or Wincy is a portrait of him- or herself, he or she is gravely mistaken, for the Turners are all creatures of the imagination. Nor are the Hilliards any particular foster-parents. If they were, we could not penetrate their disguise, for we see nothing of them but their virtues, the only qualities Wincy can remember. They must have had another side as well, though. We do not know, for instance, what Uncle Bill said when Angus almost set fire to the attic and Wincy let the pipes burst, but we strongly suspect that his first utterances were unprintable.

Only two characters—Mr. Thurman and Warden Godstow—bear any resemblance to actual persons, and this is only an inward resemblance, a reflection of their warmth and charm. Outwardly, they do not resemble the actual persons at all. In real life, Mr. Thurman is not a high school teacher. Warden Godstow is not a warden, he is not old nor unusually

9

tall, but wide, rather. At least, he was when last I saw him. That was before he undertook fire-watching from the tower of his cathedral, guarding the Kentish countryside. Perhaps with the mounting of those hundreds of steps to the top of the tower, his shape, like the shape of many other things in England, has altered, but I am certain that, like the other inward things of England, his warmth and charm have remained the same.

D. N.

Hamden, Connecticut
September 1944

April

PROLOGUE IN THE OXFORD STATION

EVEN IN the barrenness of the Oxford station, Mrs. Turner felt the push of spring. A hopeful, forward-looking spring it seemed, as she and the Professor impatiently awaited the London train. Three years before, with invasion threatening, they had sent the younger children to America for safekeeping. That year spring had been a season of decay.

Sniffing the mixture of hope and coal-gas, Mrs. Turner paced the platform. John stood still, even now assuming that annoying calm. But Mrs. Turner was not deceived. There were little beads of perspiration on his nose.

She herself felt, for some queer reason, more shaken now that Wincy and Angus were returning, than she remembered being when they left—such little souls pushing off into the world alone. It had been a tremendous risk letting them go to an unknown foster-home. They might have fallen into the hands of rough, uncultured people, or been neglected, or even ill used.

But on the contrary, judging by their letters (so many of which had been sunk that the Turners had only a misty notion of their life abroad) the children had been very happy stopping with Professor and Mrs. Hilliard of Harvard University and their young son Sutton. Life had undoubtedly been much the same for Wincy and Angus in Belmont near Cambridge, Massachusetts as it would have been in Oxford.

The Hilliards had made the most thoughtful arrangements for the children's home voyage. They had notified the Turners by cable that Wincy and Angus were travelling in the care of an Englishwoman who was returning to London. This lady had telephoned from Paddington in the early afternoon, saying that she was putting the children on the train.

Mrs. Turner thought of the forlorn figures of the children when they left. They would look different now, she knew, for they had outgrown the clothes they sailed in. But in her mind, Mrs. Turner saw the same little figures, only turned about, joyfully coming home.

The train arrived, not the tidy train of peacetime, but grimy and unswept. As people began to alight, the Turners looked anxiously up and down. Not seeing her children at once, Mrs. Turner became terrified lest they were lost.

"John, do you see them?" she asked, trying to hold back the terror.

"Not yet," Professor Turner replied calmly, turning to look in the other direction.

And then, far in the distance, Mrs. Turner caught sight of a little boy in long trousers and a shirt open at the throat.

"Oh, there's Angus at the bottom of the platform," she exclaimed. "My little lad—how he's grown! But who is the lady with him carrying a violin-case? And where's Wincy? John, your eyes are stronger than mine. Where is Wincy?"

"Yes, that's Angus," her husband said, turning around. "Looks fit, doesn't he? Who's the lady with him? Why— bless my soul!—the lady with him is Wincy."

"No, John, not the one I mean. It must be some woman who befriended them in the train. Don't you see her—in the mauve hat with ringlets brushing her shoulders like a cinema-actress? Wincy has plaits."

"She did have, you mean, when she left. That *is* Wincy, I assure you, Rachel. She's come home a grown woman."

"Nonsense," Mrs. Turner replied. "She's only fifteen."

Professor Turner had grasped his wife by the arm, unconsciously pinching it in his emotion, and was hurrying her down to the end of the platform.

And as they drew nearer, Mrs. Turner saw with her own eyes that it was, indeed, Wincy.

I

So SWIFTLY that it was like entering a new country, the haycocks, water-meadows and thatched cottages they had been journeying past, disappeared, and the spires of Oxford stretched like cut-outs across the train-window, black against the twilight.

Like floating in midstream, Wincy thought. You can see both banks. But as soon as you reach one side, you can barely see the other any more. When the train stops, America will begin to look like something I read about in a book.

Now she could see the gas-works. They dashed through a streak of smoke and then Wincy saw the spires again. She pulled her brother to the window.

"There it is, Angus—look—we're home!"

"Where?" he asked indifferently. "Just churches."

"That's Oxford, Angus. We're almost there."

She straightened his collar and tucked in his shirt and then she took a mirror from her large patent-leather purse and considered herself. Her hat looked swell, especially since she had had the permanent.

"Aw gee," Angus yawned, sprawling all over the seat, "I wish Sutty was here." He turned to the window again. "And Uncle Bill and Aunt Polly," he added dreamily.

"Don't!" Wincy cried. Then, seeing she had startled Angus, she was sorry.

But she could hardly bear any longer this homesickness for the Hilliards which she had tried to hide all the way over. She missed the kids at school, too—even Sandy Whipple, that drip the girls said had a crush on her. Now that she came to think of it, he wasn't so bad—quite decent, in fact. They had had fun at school dances and that time he took her to the Ice Carnival, when they didn't get home till midnight.

It was wrong, though, to think of American people now. Wincy shut her eyes and tried to see her parents—Mummie, slender with a pointed nose and golden hair always so beautifully brushed; Daddy, fairer than Mummie and even thinner —she could see them when she thought of each feature, but they were not real people, moving and living. Angus didn't seem to remember them at all.

As the train jerked to a standstill, the other passengers in the compartment opened the door and jumped out.

Wincy snatched up her violin-case and her purse and, holding Angus tightly by the hand, she pulled him with her out of the carriage.

They stood still for what seemed a very long time, looking about bewildered. Then Wincy saw her parents in the distance. "There they are!" she cried, happiness rushing through her so that it prickled her eyes. "There they are!"

"Is *that* them?"

"Yes. Wave."

They ran down the platform, the violin-case bouncing against Wincy's leg. And now, at last, she had her arms around her mother. This was the way she had dreamed it would be, all those long days on the boat! Daddy was waiting for his embrace, beaming at her over Mummie's head, and she turned to kiss him, noticing that his hair wasn't fair at all, the way she had remembered it, but pale silver.

Meanwhile Angus, looking a bit befuddled, had been caught up in his mother's arms. Then his father turned to him with outstretched hand.

"Welcome home, my boy," he said, his eyes crinkling as he smiled down at Angus ever so lovingly. But he betrayed no further feeling, merely shaking hands gravely with his son.

"Gee!" exclaimed Angus, standing off to inspect his father. "I didn't think you looked like that."

"Didn't you?" his father asked in the tone of voice reserved by professors for discussing the opinions of very small boys. "What had you expected?"

"Well," Angus said emphatically, "I didn't think you were a shrimp—I thought you'd be bigger than Uncle Bill."

Professor Turner's features froze and his eyes sought the horizon, which was, unfortunately, obscured by the walls of the station.

Wincy tried desperately to think of something to say. "How's Mark?"

"Very fit," Mrs. Turner replied, "judging by his last letter. He's with his squadron. Your father and I have found it very worrying, having a flyer son, but at least we have our little ones with us again."

"Little ones! Why, Mummie, I'm as tall as you now. And don't forget—Angus is nine."

"That's true, dear. Somehow, I had thought you would both come back looking very much as you did when you left. Very stupid of me, wasn't it? When the train pulled in, I looked for a little girl with plaits."

"I thought you'd be surprised," Wincy said, pleased with the effect she was making. "I got the bob just a week before we sailed. There wasn't time to write."

"And Angus," Mrs. Turner continued, running her hand over her son's crew-cut. "He's like a shorn lamb."

"It's just like Sutty's bean-shave," Angus announced proudly.

"Like a convict, I should say," put in his father. "But take heart, Rachel. Hair is one thing that can be counted upon to renew itself—at his age."

Mrs. Turner grasped Wincy's arm affectionately. "We must get the boxes out of the luggage-van," she said, leading her daughter down the platform.

Wincy looked sideways at her mother. No, that wasn't the way she had expected her to look. The features were the same, but sharper, as though someone had put accenting lines into a drawing.

Angus and his father, walking along behind, were silent. Neither of them seemed to find anything to say.

When at last all the luggage had been claimed and strapped onto a taxi and they were driving home, Professor Turner tipped back Wincy's chin and peered into her face.

"Well, chicken," he said, "you left home a little girl in a

school tunic and beaver hat and you have returned to us a grown woman."

Wincy beamed. She had been afraid that her parents might not perceive the change in her. Parents sometimes didn't. But everything was well now. *Her* parents had appreciated her immediately.

"What did they do in the States to make you age so prematurely?" the Professor asked, smiling. "It's amazing."

"Don't chivvy her, John. The unsuitable outfit makes her look old. On Monday I shall purchase some clothes appropriate to her age," Mrs. Turner announced, adding ruefully, "we'll have to use our coupons."

"Oh," exclaimed Wincy, "but I just got this suit before we left. I wanted to come home super duper. You know—smart. Aunt Polly didn't think it so becoming, but I did, so she bought it."

"It was kind of Mrs. Hilliard to go to the expense," Mrs. Turner said earnestly. "I dare say girls your age wear clothes like that in America, but here they are reserved for grown women. We consider such a large shiny purse vulgar for a girl."

Glancing from her clothes to Wincy's face, Mrs. Turner must have seen something of her daughter's disappointment, for she added in a gentler tone, "I can't quite explain it, Wincy, but in Oxford that mauve hat would identify you with a class to which you do not belong."

As a matter of fact, Wincy remembered, Aunt Polly hadn't liked the hat either, but she believed in people learning by experience. She agreed to buy the hat if Wincy promised to wear it all season, even if she tired of the gaudy color. It was a grown-up agreement. Now that the hat had failed to impress her parents as she had meant it to do, Wincy was no longer sure that she did fancy it, but she had promised to wear it and she would.

"Next season I'll try to pick one that pleases you," she told her mother meekly.

"No, my dear. You will get another hat on Monday—something appropriate to your years. I shall choose it for you."

That was just what Nannie used to say when they were asked out to tea. Nannie, in her brown uniform, would push Angus in the pram to keep his shoes clean, and Wincy, walking beside her, wondered whether there would be Dundee or Banbury cake for tea. But when the platter was at last within reach, Nannie, murmuring something about their digestion, would gently push Wincy and Angus aside with her brown elbows saying, "I shall choose one for you."

They had reached Banbury Road and stopped before the house. Wincy could make out familiar shapes behind the brick wall—the arched doorway, the bow-window of the dining room, the cowls and chimney-pots.

But these were merely shapes. It was her mother's last sentence, reminding Wincy of Nannie's determined brown arms, their warm unyielding safeness, which gave the house life. Hearing it, Wincy knew she had come home.

II

THERE WAS a blue sticker in the bow-window, and as she rushed up the path, Wincy made out the letters W.V.S.

Something to do with Mummie's war job, she supposed,

but Wincy wasn't going to stop and remark about that now, for she couldn't wait to see the interior of the house. Her father was fussing with the keys. He was so slow, and she felt so impatient. . . .

"Is Nannie here?" Angus asked.

"No. Nannie left soon after you sailed," his mother explained. "Don't you remember, my boy? I wrote you about it. She was dreadfully upset for fear strangers wouldn't give you proper care."

Angus seemed to think this very funny. "The poor fish—" he remarked.

Mrs. Turner looked at him in a puzzled way.

Let us in, please let us in, Wincy was saying inside her head, as they stood before the closed door.

But first her parents carefully cleaned their shoes on the scraper. Angus, fascinated, tried it, too.

"Goofy," said Wincy. "You've barely set foot in the street since we left Boston."

At last the door was opened. Professor Turner walked in and Wincy followed.

Though it was dearly familiar, everything seemed smaller than she had expected. There above the umbrella-stand was the hatrack with Daddy's mack and Burberry and even the old gas-masks hanging from its branching arms. There was the monk's bench, where she and Angus had been made to sit on muddy days while they waited for Nannie to wheel the pram around.

Then Angus had his first flash of recognition. On the journey he had complained that he didn't remember anything about Oxford except Nannie. Now, seeing the monk's bench, he looked under the seat. Then he straightened up again, audibly disappointed.

"What's wrong, my boy?" his father asked.

"I thought under there was where we used to keep Duffy's leash."

"So it was," Professor Turner said. "But when Duffy was put to sleep, the leash was thrown in the dustbin. Your mother and I couldn't bear to see it."

Poor Angus, Wincy thought, watching his face. He and Duffy were pups together. Mummie had written once that it was impossible to feed dogs properly in wartime, but even Wincy had forgotten.

The dining room looked just the same, with the white bellpull hanging over a bowl of cherry blossoms in the center of the table. When she was very small, Wincy thought the walls were painted with melted chocolate and she licked them once to find out. But Cook had happened in, and she had had her mouth washed out with soap.

"Smells different here," Angus said, wrinkling his nose as they stood in the passage.

Wincy noticed the same thing. "Coal-gas," she explained, "and flowers."

"And cabbage," Angus added. "In Belmont it was onions."

"And steam-heat," Wincy went on, "you could smell it coming up in the radiators."

Professor Turner settled himself in the drawing room. His wife led Angus up to the nursery, but Wincy lingered happily on the stairs, noticing that the water-pails and sand-buckets were still about, though they had removed them in Belmont.

In the nursery everything looked exactly as it had done when she and Angus left. There was Nannie's rush-seated chair by the high fireguard and the railed-off space next to the chimney-breast, where Angus used to be put for safe-keeping. On the dwarf-table in the window-recess stood a jar of daffs and also, as if Wincy and Angus had never been away, a tray of milk, biscuits and damsons—nursery-supper waiting for them.

Angus, who had found the provisions on the journey distressingly inadequate, made straight for it, and wolfed his share standing up. Then he proceeded to unpack his bag, strewing the contents on the cork carpet. He was soon sitting in the centre of a pile of underwear, fishing-tackle, and balsa-wood.

"What's that, dear?" Mrs. Turner asked, as Angus began undoing a bundle carefully swathed in layers of handkerchiefs.

"The nightingale," he said, producing a little metal bird. It perched over a cup pierced by a tiny rubber tube. Angus ran to the wash-basin and returned blowing a shrill, warbling sound, that was supposed to imitate the song of the nightingale. He stood before his mother showing off.

"Lovely, darling," she said, "but you're drooling dreadfully."

"It's okay," Angus assured her, taking the tube out of his mouth and wiping his chin on the shoulder of his shirt. "I always do. Isn't it snazzy? Uncle Bill let me take it home—it really belongs to the *Toy Symphony*."

"What's that?"

"You know—that Symphony with the toy instruments—cuckoo and quail and trumpet. We played it all the time.

Wincy, what's the name of the guy who wrote the *Toy Symphony?*"

"Haydn."

"Haydn," Angus repeated, awaiting a sign of recognition from his mother, but she still looked blank. "I used to play the nightingale part. I liked it so much, Uncle Bill let me have it."

"It's very nice," Mrs. Turner said politely.

"You ain't kidding!" Angus exclaimed.

"Pardon me, dear?"

Although his mother looked perplexed, Angus did not seem to know how to answer, for he went on blowing.

Wincy did not unpack. She was less eager to see the things she had brought with her than the ones she had left behind. They were stored in a cupboard between the windows. The door of the cupboard had never shut properly and Nannie had had to lean Mark's cricket bat against it. Although Wincy had forgotten all about it, she was happy now to find the bat still there.

"Look, Angus," she called, removing the bat and opening the cupboard, "here's your golliwogg. And your trumpet and drum."

There was a row of dolls on the top shelf. Wincy took each one down, looked it over, and put it back. Could she ever have been young enough to care for dolls?

"I've brought you a present, Mummie," Angus announced, hunting through a pile of blue jeans. He pulled out a box and handed it proudly to his mother.

"To think," she exclaimed, smiling as she took the box, "that my little son is old enough to go on a journey and bring back a present for me—" But she looked startled when she saw a huge, turbaned Negress grinning at her from the wrapper.

"What—what is it?"

"Flapjacks!" Angus announced triumphantly, waiting for a delighted response.

"What are they?"

"Wait till breakfast and you'll find out," Angus promised, stroking his stomach and smacking his lips. "Boy, you should see me and Sutty shovel them away— And look," he extricated a tin from a bundle of sweatshirts, "maple syrup! Uncle Bill brought it from Vermont. We saved it for you."

"It's like treacle," Wincy explained, opening her suitcase. "Here's my present for you, Mummie."

She had brought her mother a pale blue cardigan.

Pleasure illuminated Mrs. Turner's face. "How lovely!" she exclaimed. "It would take ever so many coupons in England. I do so wish Mark could see it—the last time he was home, he remarked how shabby my Fair Isle was getting."

One of her presents, at least, had been a success, Wincy gloated to herself. Happiness sprang in her toes as she ran down to the drawing room with her father's parcel under her arm. But as she handed him her present, she felt suddenly small and shy.

It was *Fantasia*, with musical themes and Walt Disney's pictures splashed across the pages. Every time she had gone to the Harvard "Coop" she had looked at it longingly. It was expensive, but she was so determined to bring her father something he would really love, that in the end she had bought it.

Professor Turner glanced at the pictures of mushrooms

in coolie hats, Mickey Mouse as the "Sorcerer's Apprentice," the dinosaurs and dancing milkweed-seeds, and it was clear to Wincy that he wondered what he, Fellow in Classics at St. James's College, Oxford, could possibly have to do with these things.

"The film played in Oxford," Professor Turner said. "I believe Mark saw it when he was home on leave. A very pretty picture-book," he added, ruffling the pages and, Wincy thought, missing the point altogether.

But Wincy kept her eyes on his face until he came to Beethoven's *Pastoral Symphony*, as interpreted by Walt Disney. Slowly his expression changed. He smiled at the baby unicorns frisking around the piping faun and laughed outright at Mrs. Pegasus and the flying colts.

"These centaurettes, Wincy, remind me of you," he exclaimed gaily. "See this one with the flying plaits—that is precisely the way you looked before you went to Belmont. And this one—all over ringlets—is the way you look now. A transmogrification!"

With a mischievous smile, he looked up at her, automatically turning the page, but when he looked down again and saw the Disney Dionysius riding on a mulicorn, he became angry.

"This is simply shocking!" he said. "Instead of a god, your American artist has drawn an inebriated creature, whose foolish face and fat, pink arms remind me of the keeper of the public house in the Iffley Road. I do not hold with flippancy concerning the Greek gods, although some of the orgiastic rites connected with the worship of Dionysius *are* difficult to countenance."

He looked at Wincy's face and his manner changed. "Forgive me, my dear, for speaking my mind. I am truly pleased that you have chosen this for me, with its classical allusions, however vulgar."

"I thought you'd like it," Wincy said, but she really didn't think so any more.

"Even when you were quite a baby," her father went on, "I used to recite Greek poetry to you when you were brought down after tea. It seemed to soothe and please you." He looked at Wincy thoughtfully. "I very much deplore the fact that you did not study Greek or at least Latin in your American school. It was—I shall say it openly—a matter of great distress to me that Professor and Mrs. Hilliard did not consider your welfare in this regard, although they did everything else necessary for your well-being."

"It wasn't the Hilliards' fault, Daddy. Please don't think that. I could have elected Latin at Agassiz, only then I wouldn't have had time for physics and chemistry."

"Chemistry," he repeated, with evident distaste. "That is Professor Hilliard's field and you have been influenced by him."

Angus burst into the drawing room with a package for his father, followed by Mrs. Turner, still wearing her new cardigan.

"Chemistry," Professor Turner repeated, "well, we shall talk about that when Michaelmas term starts. We're not bothering to send you until the autumn—there are only a few weeks left to Trinity."

"Look at the lovely cardigan I have," Mrs. Turner said, holding out her arm so that her husband could see the quality of the wool.

Angus, meanwhile, had laid the package on his father's

knees, and was pulling at the wrapping in his eagerness to see him open it.

"For me, is it? What fortunate parents we are, Rachel! Not only have our children returned to us; they have come bearing gifts."

This was something very special. For weeks before sailing, Angus had struggled to think of a suitable gift. He hadn't really remembered his father, he had only known him from the large photograph in the leather frame that stood on his bedside-table. It was such a large photograph that Angus had got the impression his father was a sort of superman, and what could a superman wish for?

He had looked about at the things in Uncle Bill's study, asking himself whether his father would like any of them. Over the mantel above the fireplace hung the airplane model that Sutty and Angus had made, with a good deal of help from Uncle Bill. If he brought a model-kit to his father, they could build the plane together, he told Wincy. That was what Sutty did with his father.

"I don't really believe Daddy will care for it," Wincy had warned.

But Angus had made up his mind. "That's the kind of thing men like, fathers and professors," he stated flatly. "I'm going to get it."

Could he afford a kit like that? It would cost seventy-five cents. After buying the pancake-flour, he had only about half a dollar left. Wincy offered to pay part of it, but Angus wanted to buy the present all by himself. He went to Aunt Polly for a pay-job. She found that the cellar-windows were badly in need of washing. Angus did them, pocketed his quarter, and went off on his bike to Harvard Square to get the model-kit. It was a beauty, it really was.

As his father opened the box and everything lay open to view—the plans, the balsa boards with the outline of the wings, the nose-block, propeller, and landing-gear—Angus could barely keep from pulling the parts out and setting them up.

But Professor Turner examined the markings on the balsa boards in utter bewilderment. He had never made things with his hands like Uncle Bill. Wincy doubted if he could. He did know, however, how to steer the subject to familiar ground. "It was Daedalus," he told Angus, "who invented the first aircraft, fashioning wings of wax and feathers. He and his son Icarus attempted to fly with them. But Icarus flew too near the sun. His wings melted and he fell into the sea."

"What a sap!" Angus remarked. Then, his attention returning to the model-kit, he took out a little tube. "Look," he said, holding it under his father's nose. "Dope."

"*Dope*, Angus?" his mother inquired, her voice rising.

"Yes," said Angus. "It's better than glue for sticking celluloid."

Mrs. Turner smiled, perceiving her mistake, but then a worried look crept into her face.

"John, I quite forgot, in my excitement over the children's arrival—" she looked at her husband anxiously, "the Warden wishes to see you tonight."

"Bother!"

"Do you suppose it's one of those Undergraduate Approach things again?"

"Shouldn't wonder. We've already had three of the beastly

things this week," the Professor said bitterly. "Tempest in a teapot, I call it."

"Oh, John, I can't think why the College is making such a to-do. After all, you've been teaching classics for the past thirty years. My dear, I do so wish I could help you." She looked at her husband tenderly.

A wave of recognition passed over Wincy, as she watched her mother's face. Aunt Polly had looked that way, exactly, when Uncle Bill came home from the lab worried about the way an experiment was going. And yet, they didn't look one bit alike, Aunt Polly and her mother. It was just that secret lovingness.

"You won't go, will you—tonight, when we've only just come home?" Angus asked, looking up from the working-drawings of the plane with a troubled face. "I wanted to watch you make the model."

"I fear I must, Angus," his father said bleakly. "It's a frightfully important College matter."

"We could do it around nine," Angus suggested. "When will you be back?"

"Nine!" Mrs. Turner exclaimed. "You'll be long asleep by then, Angus."

"It will be nearly midnight before I return," the Professor said, sighing. "I've Home Guard after I've seen the Warden. Some other time, perhaps, my boy—" His voice trailed off. He looked worried and remote.

Wincy noticed that although her father appeared calm, little beads of perspiration were forming on his nose. She wondered what could be wrong, but did not dare to ask. Instead, to cheer everyone, she remarked on the huge pile of socks that Mrs. Turner was darning. Holes in husbands' socks, she thought, are always good for a laugh.

"How fast Daddy gets holes in his socks—" she said, making a comical face.

"They're none of them Daddy's," her mother answered gravely. "They belong to the soldiers. The W.V.S. does all the mending for the Army."

"Who's W.V.S.?" Angus asked.

"Goofy," Wincy said to him. "Mummie wrote us all about it when we were in Belmont. Don't you remember? It stands for Women's Voluntary Services."

"Right you are!" Mrs. Turner exclaimed, looking up proudly from her mending. "They call us 'the second line of civil defense.'"

There was silence for a moment. Mrs. Turner was rolling the socks into pairs and the Professor was staring out of the window.

"Say," Angus asked suddenly, "when do we eat?"

"But you've had your supper, my dear boy," his mother answered.

"What—that snack? No Mummie, I mean when do we have dinner—you know, all of us in the dining room."

"In England children your age do not have dinner in the dining room. At that hour they are in bed. A quiet nursery-supper, such as you have already had, is much the best for the digestion."

"Rats on the digestion. I'm hungry," Angus said. "Sutty and us always had our meals in the dining room with Uncle Bill and Aunt Polly."

"Shocking language you've learned in the States, my boy," Professor Turner remarked.

"Mummie dear," Wincy put in, coming to Angus's aid, "we don't have to go back to the old nursery-ways, do we—now that Angus is a big boy and I'm grown up? It would be humiliating."

"Not nursery-ways, pet—of course not," Mrs. Turner said, stroking the hair back from Wincy's forehead and looking fondly into her eyes. "We couldn't possibly carry on as before without Nannie. But in matters of supper, and so on, now that you are home again, you must do as other children do in England."

III

THERE WAS a soft thudding on the stairs. Wincy, who had been reading mystery stories on the homeward voyage, awoke the next morning with the certainty that a body was being smuggled out of the house.

For a minute, before she remembered that she was back in Oxford, she listened for the buzz of Uncle Bill's electric razor. When it stopped, she could get into the bathroom. There was that thud again, but louder this time, then silence. The body had landed at the bottom of the stairs.

Wincy rushed out and looked over the banisters. There on the last step was a sheet-covered ghost, wrestling with a mattress. At the sound of footsteps, Angus looked up, fear in his eyes. No wonder, after the indelicate and quite unnecessary remarks that wretched stewardess had made . . .

"Is it Hallowe'en?" Wincy asked, laughing. "Before I opened my eyes, I thought a body was being dragged out of the house under cover of darkness. Wait a minute and I'll help."

"Good morning, children," Mrs. Turner called gaily, emerging from the scullery. "Dear me—Angus, what is this?"

"Such a big mattress," Angus remarked, tugging furiously. "The one in Belmont, I could manage that alone easy. Say, have you got one of those pulley lines, the way we have? You hang up the sheet at one end and pull it, and zip!—it's down at the other."

"But why should you wish to take your bedding into the garden?" Mrs. Turner asked. "We always air it at the window in the bedroom. That is quite sufficient in this climate."

"It's wet," Wincy explained, trying to give her mother the knowing look which passes between grown-ups.

"Do you mean—? Angus, how shocking! A boy of nine— Why, even as a little chap you never did a thing like that. At least," Mrs. Turner added a little uncertainly, "Nannie never mentioned it."

That dreadful look was in Angus's face again. Wincy wished people would stop harping on this business and give the kid a chance. You wouldn't expect a stewardess to understand about child psychology, the way Uncle Bill and Aunt Polly did, but surely Mummie must.

"Has this been going on all the time that you were stopping with the Hilliards?" Mrs. Turner asked.

"Oh, no!" Wincy assured her.

"Dear me, Angus," Mrs. Turner concluded wearily, "you had better air your pyjamas as well."

Angus shook his head.

"Do as you are told, Angus," his mother urged.

"But I didn't wear them."

"You *didn't*?" Mummie cried. She was shocked. "Oh, Angus, what shall I do with you? If you are going to be tiresome, we'll never manage without a governess."

"I'm not tiresome, Mummie. You just don't understand how we do. Sutty Hilliard and I always sleep raw in the summertime—it makes men tough."

"That, then, is the cause of your trouble," Mrs. Turner announced, and she seemed relieved. "You have taken cold in the bladder. Peg the linen on the lines, then. Don't look disturbed, my boy. We'll soon have you right. A flannel band—"

Before her mother could say any more, Wincy pushed the sheet-draped Angus out into the garden.

The grass felt lovely between her toes. Everything was in its proper place, just the way it had always been—wallflowers and alyssum in the border, the great oaktree at the bottom of the garden, in which Mark used to play, and Daddy's peartree growing up the wall.

Wincy and Angus had put the bedding in the sun and were chasing round the house when Wincy heard her mother's voice.

"Do come in, child," she called. "Naughty thing, frisking about in your night things publicly," she said, smiling while she reproved. "Brekker is almost ready, anyhow."

"Oh," exclaimed Wincy. "Sorry. I'll be down in two shakes and help."

When she had dressed, she found Angus already in the kitchen, rooting about for a skillet.

"Mind the stove, Angus," Mrs. Turner warned. "I shouldn't come too close."

"Nuts!" he replied. "I'll just fry us up some flapjacks."

"Need you talk so loud, dear?"

The Professor had come down and was standing in the doorway, watching Angus grease the pan with a wad of paper. He looked tired after his night's work. "Splendid weather," he remarked, patting each child on the shoulder.

"Yes," said Wincy. "Your peartree looks fine, Daddy."

Angus was singing as he stood over the pan.

"Mammy's little baby loves shortnin', shortnin',
Mammy's little baby loves shortnin' bread."

"Are you certain you know the proper thing to do?" his mother asked, eyeing Angus nervously. "I should never have thought a boy of nine could be experienced in cookery."

"Wait till I flip 'em!" Angus shouted. "Boy, you should see Uncle Bill—he flips 'em so high, they just miss the ceiling. He's a wiz!"

Mrs. Turner dropped into Cook's chair.

"It has been very difficult for me since the maids left," she said, and Wincy could see she was very tired. "Cook was with us twenty years, and in that time I seldom entered the kitchen."

"We'll fix things," Angus promised. He was beating the batter. "We're not used to any old cooks."

"Didn't the Hilliards have servants at all?" Mrs. Turner inquired with surprise. "I knew they had no nannie, but wasn't there a cook?"

"Of course not," Angus replied disdainfully. "We didn't need any of those old women fussing at us. Aunt Polly just tacked our house-jobs on the bulletin-board and then we knew what to do."

"Just at first," Wincy remembered, "it was rather difficult. I was always dropping plates."

"We caught on pretty soon, though," Angus assured them.

"By the by, Rachel," Professor Turner put in, "do write to Mrs. Hilliard and thank her for all she and Professor Hilliard have done for our children."

"Yes, John, I mean to. I *feel* very grateful, but I don't know how to express the feeling in a letter. You could do it better, I know."

"Not at all," Professor Turner replied. "This sort of letter comes most naturally from the mother."

Wincy was standing by the scullery-window, looking into the garden and thinking of the happy time in Belmont.

"We were such babies when we got there," she said. "I couldn't even comb my hair and Angus just stood with his arms stretched out waiting for someone to put clothes on him."

"I suppose it was a mistake," Mrs. Turner said thoughtfully, "Nannie's never allowing you to dress yourselves. She felt that you were too inexpert and slow. You were beautifully turned out, but now I see it was a poor preparation for your American experience and trying for Mrs. Hilliard."

"It never occurred to us that the Hilliards would not have plenty of servants," Professor Turner added. "Had we known the way things were, we should never have been willing to impose upon them."

"But it was of their own choosing," Mrs. Turner argued. "They went to the committee that took care of the British children and offered their home. I often wondered why they did it."

Angus, pouring the batter into the pan, looked around, surprised. "They liked us," he explained.

"Of course they did, my love. But I mean, the extra trouble

—to say nothing of the expense. The Hilliards had never heard of us. They couldn't have known beforehand that they were going to like you. Many people here in Oxford have found the evacuees extremely tiresome."

"Oh, sure," said Angus, "evacuees—that's different. But us—" He grasped the pan with both hands. "Watch now—I'm going to flip!"

Terror passed over his mother's face as, with a quite unnecessary flourish, Angus sent the pancake flying out of the skillet. But it was not for nothing, the many times he had helped prepare breakfast in the Hilliard kitchen and over the campfire. With striking coolness, he recovered the pancake, golden side up, and his mother rewarded him with a look of the most profound respect.

IV

"Ah-h!" exclaimed Professor Turner when they were at breakfast. "Nectar and ambrosia! I never tasted anything so delicately flavoured."

Angus was bursting with pride. He said nothing, but the very silence was an indication of his joy.

"Since you are still tired from the journey," Mrs. Turner announced, "we shan't go to church. Besides," she added to her husband in a lower tone, "I must get the children properly fitted out before they are seen—specially Wincy."

"Is it Sunday?" Wincy asked. "I'd forgotten. All the days seem alike on board ship."

"Sunday was a beautiful day in Belmont," Angus said

dreamily. "We used to go hiking or hunting wildflowers or skiing. We had supper at the Suttons, or they came to our house. Afterwards we played in Uncle Bill's orchestra."

"I didn't realize you had mastered an instrument, too, Angus," his father said.

"Sure, I played the cymbals or the rattle. Uncle Harley mostly played the rattle, though. Just think, he's never learned to play anything else in all these years—" Angus giggled.

"I should think, since he isn't musical, that Doctor Sutton would prefer to listen," Professor Turner said.

"Oh, no, nobody listens," Angus explained earnestly, "not even visitors. Uncle Bill says the noise would kill 'em."

"Sunday seems to have been very pleasant in Belmont," Mrs. Turner said, "but didn't you go to church?"

"Never was time," Wincy said casually.

"Yes, we did, Wincy," Angus insisted. "We always went to church Christmas and Easter."

Mrs. Turner's eyes darkened for a moment, but she changed the subject. "Do tell me, Angus," she asked, "do you still have your herd of imaginary cows?"

"What cows?"

"They played a big part in your life at one time," Mrs. Turner explained, smiling. "You had a pretend dairy in the park and Nannie said you always used to talk to the cows perfectly seriously."

"I remember now," Wincy said. "But Angus never played that in Belmont."

"Mummie cow often had breakfast in bed," Mrs. Turner recalled. "The maid cows took it up to her. And Nannie cow was run over by a bus."

"Are you kidding?" Angus asked.

"Am I what, dear?"

"Are you kidding?" he asked again, shaking his head incredulously. "Was I ever that dumb?"

"Just wishful thinking," Wincy reassured him. Her father looked at her in a puzzled way and she wondered why.

"Children dear," Mrs. Turner announced, "I've planned rather a jolly surprise for you."

Angus looked up instantly in happy expectation.

"To celebrate your return, we're having the Quelches for tea—you're to have it with us in the drawing room."

"Quelches!" Angus repeated. "What are Quelches? Something like doughnuts?"

"Don't shout so, Angus dear," Mrs. Turner begged.

"You don't remember the Quelches?" his father asked, surprised and a little reproachful. "Quelch is a Senior Fellow at St. James's."

"You used to be so sweet together when you were very little—you and Mark and the two little Quelches," Mrs. Turner recalled, "all sitting round the nursery-table being fed by the two nannies." Wincy noticed that when she spoke of the past, her mother's face brightened and became quite beautiful.

"Francis is two years younger, than Mark," Mrs. Turner went on, "but Brenda is exactly your age, Wincy. You were born the same week and were always such friends."

"I remember them," Wincy said. "Francis was an awful pest. He used to pull my braids."

"Yes, he was quite a naughty little boy," Mrs. Turner admitted, "but you'll find Francis well behaved now. He's going up to St. James's in the autumn."

"If he can pass in the Latin paper," Professor Turner added dubiously.

"Boys always seem to have trouble with Latin," Wincy observed. "Sandy Whipple had a terrible time."

"Who?" Mrs. Turner asked. "I don't remember hearing about him in your letters."

"Just a boy in Belmont," Wincy explained.

"Indeed?" Mrs. Turner remarked with a queer note in her voice. Then she added, in some disappointment, "I thought you would be impatient to see Brenda as soon as you arrived."

"Haven't seen her for ages," Wincy murmured without interest.

"Yes," Mrs. Turner said, the happy light coming into her face again, "but I can still picture you going to school, walking hand in hand down Banbury Road in your blue tunics and beaver hats, followed by the two nannies in their brown Norland uniforms. It was a lovely sight."

Either because he felt out of things, not being able to remember the people who were being discussed, or because he was ashamed of having mistaken them for something to eat, Angus made up a little singsong.

"Quel-chy, Quel-chy, Quel-chy," he sang.

"Do stop, Angus," his father commanded. "You are very rude. Quelch is quite the coming man in our College. I shouldn't be surprised," he added, hoping to impress Angus with Doctor Quelch's importance, "I shouldn't be surprised to see him become Warden some day."

Angus stopped singing, stuffed in the last mouthful and got down from the table. "I'll wash up," he announced.

"And I'll dry," Wincy said.

"I was going to—" Mrs. Turner began, looking surprised.

"Oh, no, Mummie, you were setter."

Angus was figuring things out. "That leaves you the retriever, Daddy," he declared.

"Leaves me what?" his father asked in a startled tone.

"You clear the table," Angus explained. "In Belmont we had two trays, one had a picture of a setter painted on it and one a retriever. The guy who set the table used the setter tray and the guy who cleared used the retriever. See?"

"You want me to be a retriever?" Professer Turner asked in amazement. He stood in the doorway, his arms dangling from their shoulder-sockets and looked as if he had been invited to climb a tree. "Actually, I don't know how—," he protested. "Besides, I've fire-watching this morning."

"Doing housework alone is drudgery," Wincy explained to him, as she took the dripping dishes from Angus's hands. "But when everyone pitches in, it's fun. We used to have some of our best times in the kitchen in Belmont."

"You bet," Angus agreed. "Uncle Bill would put a saucepan on his head and dance a jig and sometimes we'd all sing rounds or those chorale things while we cleaned up. Now Daddy, you just take the oleo and the milkjug. Put them in the larder and wipe up the crumbs."

To Wincy's amazement, her father did as he was told.

Mrs. Turner smiled tolerantly, but she did not look altogether pleased. "Many of the men we know are helping with the washing up since the war," she said. "I've never liked it, though. I don't hold with having a don in the scullery."

V

"HIT THE line! C'mon team, *smash'm—*"

Wincy smiled as these un-English yells came in from the garden, where Angus was kicking his football. Then she leaned out of the scullery-window.

"Turn it down," she advised, laughing. "They may fuss about football on Sunday. Things are different here."

"You're telling me!" Angus answered.

Wincy looked about the kitchen to see whether there was anything more to do before the guests arrived. The loaf had been sliced, the tea-caddy stood ready, the crumpets were arranged on the platter.

But the tray didn't look nice, Wincy thought, because the cups and saucers were so frightful. No two seemed to match and some of them were as thick as the ones in the cafeteria near Harvard Square. Mrs. Turner had always been so proud of her Spode tea-things. Evidently another of those changes brought about by the war—they turned up in such unexpected places.

From the passage Wincy could see into the drawing room. Her father was reading and her mother was sitting at the writing-table in her new cardigan composing that difficult letter to Aunt Polly. A photograph of Mark in his R.A.F. uniform stood on the writing-table over the shelf where the blue notepaper was kept, and on either side of it was one of Wincy and of Angus which Aunt Polly had had taken in Cambridge the first year they were there. Wincy remembered how carefully she had wrapped them to send to Professor and Mrs. Turner for Christmas and how relieved they all were when they heard months later that the pictures had arrived.

It was really a friendly room, with the chintz-covered arm-chairs, jars of flowers on the mantel shelf, and the French windows opening out into the garden. Why had it always frightened Wincy when, in her smocked Liberty print, she was brought down after tea to spend an hour with her parents?

Professor Turner, glancing up from his book, saw Wincy standing in the passage and blinked, not yet accustomed to her presence.

"Wincy, my dear," he called, shutting the book over his finger, "we haven't yet heard you play. Do give us a tune."

This was it. This was what she had been waiting for—the chance to show her parents what she had learned in Bel-mont, she, Wincy, the first Turner to play an instrument. Which would they prefer, she wondered, the Händel or the Mozart Sonata?

"Yes, dear, do play something," Mrs. Turner urged a trifle absently, for she was still struggling with the letter.

Wincy fetched her case and opened it. There lay the precious fiddle, wrapped in a length of pink material. As she unwound it, Wincy held the material up by one corner.

"What do you think this is?" she asked, laughing.

Professor Turner took the material in his hand and ex-amined it. "Silk, I should say," he guessed, "used to protect the instrument."

"But what do you suppose it was before? When Uncle Bill bought the fiddle, it hadn't anything around it, so Aunt Polly went to her piece-bag and this is what she pulled out—part of her old slip!"

Professor Turner dropped the silk as though he had suddenly found it infected. His face froze the way it had done in the station yesterday. In Belmont they had all laughed when Aunt Polly pulled the material out of her piece-bag.

Queer, Wincy thought, screwing up the bow. She held the nut to her eye and squinted down the length of the stick to see whether the dampness on board ship had warped it. Then she took up the fiddle and tuned it, bowing the strings in pairs.

Now she was no longer in Oxford, nor even in Belmont, but deep in some lucid pool of sound, the hollow, unmixed intervals vibrating in widening circles around her. This was not a mechanical preliminary to music, but part of the music itself—a prelude, fifth following fifth, something Bach might have used to begin a suite.

A loud clanging suddenly drowned it out.

Wincy's bow arm dropped. Her mind rushed back from the prelude in fifths to the room in which she was standing. Her parents, whom she had forgotten, were waiting for her to begin a piece.

Now they jumped up and hurried out into the passage.

Angus came running in. "Shucks!" he exclaimed.

Wincy hung back in the drawing room, putting the fiddle away, and Angus kept close beside her. They could hear their parents and the visitors all talking at once. Then Mrs. Turner drew Wincy and Angus into the passage to be presented.

"There you are at last, you poor children," Mrs. Quelch exclaimed in a high-pitched voice. "How you've grown, all this nasty long time out of England!"

"It wasn't nasty," Angus protested instantly. "It was swell."

Mrs. Quelch gave a well-bred snicker at his flat pronunciation of the word "nasty."

Right then, Wincy decided that she didn't care for this lady. But her father had seemed anxious to impress the Quelches and so she put in primly, "Angus and I are jolly glad to be home."

Doctor Quelch turned to Angus. He was a tall man with an important-looking nose. "See any Indians, young chap?" he asked, playfully poking Angus in the solar-plexus.

"Nope."

"Any cow-catchers?" the Doctor went on.

"Say, we weren't out West," Angus told him. "We were in Massachusetts."

"Quite," Doctor Quelch remarked. "It's all one to me—all those states. No Indians in Massachusetts, I gather. Thoroughly civilized—"

Professor Turner came forward. "They were in Belmont on the outskirts of Cambridge," he explained, "stopping with a Harvard professor."

"Quite," Doctor Quelch repeated. "It's a strange thing, Turner," he observed, changing from the voice he used when addressing children to his natural one, "but whenever I hear the name Cambridge, I assume that it refers to our sister university. It always takes me a moment to recollect that it is also the name of a city in the States."

He laughed heartily, but Wincy couldn't see what was funny about being so dumb.

Francis smiled politely, following Professor Turner into the drawing room. He was a tall, good-looking fellow with nice eyes and a handsome nose, like his father's, but Wincy thought if he enjoyed his father's joke, he must be a drip.

She took Brenda's coat and hung it on one of the branching arms. Then, smiling into Brenda's scared little rabbit-face, Wincy drew her into the drawing room.

"We used to go to Newfields together," Wincy began. "Remember? Do you still go there?"

"Yes," said Brenda, dropping her eyes.

"I'm going there next term," Wincy continued. "I guess it'll be very strange after Agassiz—that was my school in America. Are you taking physics or chemistry?"

"No," said Brenda.

Well, Brenda might be fifteen too, but she acted like one of the sixth grade kids at Agassiz.

Offering Doctor Quelch a cigarette, Professor Turner sat down beside him on the oak settle. "Roaring gale we had last night, wasn't it?" he remarked.

"Touch of north in it," Doctor Quelch said. "Great pity it's turned so cold—the plum is well out and likely to be damaged."

"So it may," Professor Turner answered gravely. "But I think the apple blossom is just safe—just."

"Planted your broad beans yet, Turner?" Doctor Quelch inquired.

"Yes, and early peas," the Professor replied, adding with a smile, "I also set out a battery of mousetraps."

"Success?"

"Not exactly," the Professor admitted. "That is, I caught a victim, but not a mouse. It was a chaffinch, poor thing."

The ladies had taken the chintz-covered chairs. Mrs. Quelch immediately brought out her knitting and set to work.

"Sorry we've no cakes for tea," Mrs. Turner apologized,

lighting the spirit-lamp under the silver teakettle. "I did the shops yesterday, but couldn't get any."

"They're not worth eating when one does manage to find some," Mrs. Quelch answered comfortingly. "Shopping now really is a fine art," she explained, turning to Wincy. "My dear Winifred," she rattled on in her high-pitched voice, "you can't guess how impatient your dear parents have been! All winter they've talked of nothing but your coming in April. And now, at last, April is here."

Mrs. Turner nodded, her eyes shining as she smiled lovingly on her children. She was really beautiful when she looked that way, Wincy discovered.

Across the room, Professor Turner smiled on them, too.

"Oh, to be in England," Doctor Quelch began in his teaching voice, "now that April's there—"

Wincy looked up at him swiftly. She wouldn't have recognized the line if Mr. Thurman, who taught Sophomore English at Agassiz, hadn't been a Browning fan. He had made them memorize piles of Browning, and as nobody ever did enough homework, they used to cram the poems before class, leaning against the big maple on the playground, she and Penny Poole and Brocky, who was a lot better at basketball, anyway, than at poetry.

Dear old Thurm—he was a good egg, even if he was bald and had a habit of making sarcastic remarks when kids didn't know their homework. The way he recited poetry, though, drawing out the full sound of each word, made it both musical and meaningful, and not easily forgotten.

Oh, to be in England . . . Doctor Quelch reminded Wincy of it all again, though he didn't make it sound so beautiful as Mr. Thurman used to do. To be in England . . .

Golly, Wincy thought suddenly, I *am* in England! Still, that poem only made her think of the kids at Agassiz and Mr. Thurman rolling out the words in the English Room, with the sun that came through the Brattle Street window lighting up one side of his bald head.

"I managed to get some sausage meat off the ration yesterday," Mrs. Quelch announced gloatingly.

Wincy gave a start—she had forgotten that she was home. She must stop thinking about America. The night before she and Angus left, Aunt Polly had urged her not to think of it too much, but to try to settle into life in Oxford.

"Did you *really*?" Mrs. Turner exclaimed, pouring the tea. "Lucky duck!"

Angus was passing the whole-meal bread and Wincy, remembering her part, took up the crumpets and followed round the circle. When the platters were empty, they went to the kitchen to refill them.

Even here, the sound of Mrs. Quelch's high-pitched voice penetrated. "I must say, they look well fed and singularly cheerful," she said. "I was so afraid they might have been ill-treated. Perfect strangers, you know, and foreigners to boot—"

"Where does she think we've been?" Wincy asked Angus. "In jail? She's a pill."

"Picklepuss," Angus called the lady.

Mrs. Turner was reassuring Mrs. Quelch. "Not at all," she said. "They seem to have had a very agreeable stay. Some things seem a trifle—" she hesitated, "odd, but we'll have them right in no time," she added cheerfully.

"I *am* so relieved," Mrs. Quelch said, though she sounded faintly disappointed. Canon Harcourt's children had a shocking experience—simply shocking. "Some of those Americans—"

"Yes, I know," Mrs. Turner said, loyally cutting the unpleasant remark short. "Wincy and Angus were very fortunate."

Wincy knew, too, about the Harcourt children. They had been evacuated on the same boat. They had had bad luck with their foster-parents. So had Evelyn Derby. She had gone to live with some people in Boston who sometimes invited Wincy to play with her. They were kind, but very queer people, not at all like the Hilliards, for they didn't treat Evelyn like a person, but like a new ornament for their home. At the beginning, that is—before they got fed up with her.

"It must be tiresome for you after the years of freedom," Mrs. Quelch was saying to Mrs. Turner. "You ought to listen to the talks on mothercraft until you have your hand in. I always do."

Mrs. Turner laughed. "Those wouldn't help me, I fear, so much as clothing coupons, Monica. The clothes the children brought back have such a foreign air. But I do think their accent is charming, don't you, with just that little American touch?"

Mrs. Quelch did not reply, but it was quite plain that she did not think so.

"To be sure," Mrs. Turner admitted, "those slang expressions are frightful. I can barely understand Angus half the time."

"Dear me!" exclaimed Mrs. Quelch sympathetically.

Francis broke in upon the ladies' conversation. "Look here, Mrs. Turner," he said, "you ought to go to the flicks. You'd catch on to American slang fast enough there."

Wincy, coming in with the platter, looked up to see how her mother was taking this suggestion, but she never found out, for Francis caught her eye and winked. He wasn't such a drip as she first thought.

"How poised Winifred is," Mrs. Quelch remarked, looking up. "She seems quite at home amongst grown people, not mousey and gawky, like most girls her age."

"Yes, Wincy has been in the company of older people a great deal, I gather," Mrs. Turner said, looking much pleased by the compliment. "You have no idea how handy they both are. Their foster-mother taught them to consider housekeeping fun—"

"Housekeeping fun?" Mrs. Quelch repeated, her voice higher than ever. "Fancy anything so ridiculous—"

"Yes, fun," Mrs. Turner insisted, sounding a little injured. She did wish to convince Mrs. Quelch. "All the family seems to do the work together out there and they make a game of it. This morning the children even induced their father to be the retriever. It's going to be a great help to me without Cook. Nevertheless, I do wish I had Nannie."

"I wonder what sort of people these American foster-mothers are," Mrs. Quelch said dreamily, sucking on a knitting-pin. "They sound rather like superior nannies with husbands."

On the other side of the drawing room, the two dons were discussing the affairs of their College. Wincy tried to hear their conversation.

"Tempest in a teapot is what I call it." Professor Turner was saying, twisting irritably on the settle.

"Signs of the times," Doctor Quelch said cynically. "Formerly undergraduates came to avail themselves of what the

Fellows offered. Now the Fellows are told what the under-graduates desire."

"It's not exactly that way, Quelch. The chaps seem to feel the need for something more than the old forms of instruction. They want weapons for life in this confused world. And I, for my part, would be only too glad to furnish them. But what more can I offer than authorized versions of the classics?" Professor Turner asked dismally.

Wincy felt Francis's eyes watching her.

"Is that your fiddle?" he asked.

Wincy nodded.

"Does she play well?" Mrs. Quelch inquired in a loud whisper of Mrs. Turner. "Children usually sound so squeaky, don't you think?"

Mrs. Turner looked blank. She had been nervously eyeing her husband, trying to overhear the dons' conversation, while pretending to give her full attention to Mrs. Quelch. "I really can't say," she replied. "We haven't heard her play anything yet."

Having given up all hope of making Brenda speak, Wincy sat on the stool, listening while her father and Doctor Quelch mapped out a strategy for the invasion of the continent. Francis listened, too, but he did not take part in the conversation.

"Sooner the better is what I say," Doctor Quelch announced, banging his fist on the arm of the settle.

"Yes," Professor Turner answered in a low voice, "since it must be done—" He slumped slightly against the back of the settle. "When the moment comes, it will be fraught with great anxiety for us," he added. "Mark's squadron will undoubtedly take part in the operations."

Nobody spoke for a moment. It was as if Mark's shadow had fallen across the room, filling it with fear.

"When we've settled the continent, we can turn our attention to the East," Doctor Quelch said at length, and he looked so fierce at the prospect that Wincy thought if the Japs could only see the Senior Fellow of St. James's, Oxford, they would quickly run along about their business. "It's high time we settled the Indian question, too," he added anxiously.

Professor Turner remarked that he wished Sir Stafford had been successful there. Doctor Quelch didn't agree.

Wincy felt a warmth surround her as she listened, a sense of being where she belonged. For this was what she was used to. In the Hilliard and Sutton households politics were constantly discussed, sometimes with sharp differences of opinion.

"We ought to have been firmer with those mischief-makers from the first," Doctor Quelch said with a bit of a temper. "Too much sentimental boggling."

"Oh, no, Doctor Quelch, we should have given India greater independence," Wincy put in earnestly. "It's just like England's colonial policy in the reign of George the Third. If she had been wiser then, the American colonies never would have rebelled. England would have saved herself two wars. And just think what a help it would have been in this one if there hadn't been all the delay in arranging for lend-lease and a unified command."

"That will do, Wincy," her father said. "Little girls don't hold political opinions."

Wincy's cheeks felt on fire. Little girls—

"They didn't make a Bolshie of you out there, did they,

my dear?" Doctor Quelch asked, laughing, but Wincy could see that he thought she had gone a bit queer.

To hide her confusion, she got up and passed the last of the crumpets. When she had made the circle, there was one left. She reached out for it, looking at Francis, who was talking to her about American swing bands, when Angus sneaked up and grabbed the crumpet from under her hand.

"You bum!" she exclaimed, good-naturedly.

Instantly she realized that something dreadful had happened. Conversation stopped. Except for Brenda, who sat looking at the floor in childish embarrassment, and Angus, who was placidly chewing his crumpet, everyone surrounded her with horrified stares.

Professor Turner put down his cup and saucer with a bang and mopped the beads of perspiration on his nose. Wincy must have upset him dreadfully, but what had she done?

Although Mrs. Turner's face was scarlet, her voice sounded quite controlled as she said firmly, "Go to your room, Wincy."

Wincy did not move. "What's the matter?" she asked. "What have I done?"

"Go to your room," Mrs. Turner repeated.

Wincy rushed across the drawing room, past Francis and Brenda, and managed to get to the stairs before the tears showed.

VI

EVERYTHING'S WRONG with me, Wincy thought, trailing up to her room. And is that Mummie's idea of a treat—having Doctor and Mrs. Picklepuss come to tea?

Francis isn't so bad—the way he told Mummie to go to the movies and then winked at me was nice, but that Brenda . . . if that's the kind of friend I had before I was evacuated, it's a good thing I went away.

She threw herself across the bed, punching the pillow. It was all so different from Sunday in Belmont. . . .

I didn't want to think about America—I wanted to be fair, she told herself. I tried to forget how homesick I am for Aunt Polly and Uncle Bill and Sally Sutton and the kids at Agassiz, and Mr. Thurman—even Miss Lowell. Who'd have thought in class that I could ever be homesick for Miss Lowell? It just shows what this has done to me—I wanted to be fair, but they *make* me wish I was back.

She shut her eyes, letting herself dream. Right now, this minute, the Hilliards and Suttons were probably cooking beans and hot dogs over a campfire somewhere in the country. Later they'd sit around, munching doughnuts and apples and singing between bites. Or perhaps they were square-dancing on the lawn to the tune of Uncle Bill's fiddle. If it rained, they'd pop corn in the fireplace, Sutty stuffing himself till he just rolled over on the floor and was still—for once.

In a few weeks, they'd be driving down to Scituate for a swim, thawing out afterwards on those beautiful golden-brown rocks.

Sometimes they had had to stay home on Sunday because Uncle Bill had an experiment running which had to be watched. But even that was fun, for he would take Wincy and the two little boys to the lab with him. She loved the rows of sparkling flasks, retorts and pipettes cleverly put together with glass tubing.

Uncle Bill, in his tan lab coat and crew-cut, looking no older than one of his own students, would make Angus and Sutty hold their hands behind their backs so they'd be sure not to touch anything. But Wincy was allowed to handle the stopcocks and Bunsen-burner for the experiment. Even washing out the test-tubes had been fun.

Wincy thought of afternoons in winter, when they would come in from skiing or skating and fix supper either at their house or the Suttons, singing spirituals or silly songs, like "Johnny Smoker," while they did the dishes. After that came the best part of all—Uncle Bill's orchestra. She and Sally would sit together at the same stand, playing second violin.

When Uncle Bill had seen she wasn't satisfied playing a toy instrument, but was eager to learn to play the fiddle like Sally, he had bought her one and sent her to music school. At the end of her first year in Belmont, Wincy could play well enough to keep up with the orchestra.

Although Sally was two years older, she had liked Wincy right away—it wasn't just that Sally felt she had to be nice, because her father was Aunt Polly's brother.

Gosh, she had looked a baby when she arrived in Belmont, Wincy remembered, in those silly gym tunics and the smocked Libertys, with pigtails hanging to her waist. Sally had soon put her wise to the kind of clothes older girls wear. It wasn't that Sally was clothes-crazy. She simply believed that you have to think about your type, if you want other people to recognize it. For months, Sally had been after her to get a pageboy bob with curled ends, but Wincy hadn't dared to get her pigtails cut. Suddenly, one day, just before sailing she decided to do it. She had been scared in the beauty-parlour. But the result was wonderful—she looked worlds older.

When Sally outgrew her dresses, she handed them down. There were some hanging in the wardrobe now, a bit of Sally here in Oxford. Wincy especially liked the Austrian dirndl with the puffy white blouse and silver buttons on the bodice. When she had unpacked it last night, though, Mummie said it would look outlandish in Oxford.

At first, Agassiz School had seemed very queer—you could get away with whispering and didn't have to stand when you recited. Having boys in the class seemed positively dopey. But Wincy had got used to it. She loved everything about Agassiz—dear old Thurm, even Miss Lowell.

She hadn't gone goofy over the boys the way Penny Poole and Brocky did. She really didn't care for them at all—most of them were such saps. Last term, though, Sandy Whipple had started hanging around and some of the girls teased her. They said he was nuts about her. But he wasn't. He was just a nice, friendly kid, who liked hunting rocks and minerals, the way she did. They used to go out Saturday mornings with a picnic lunch, coming home in the evening all loaded down with bits of rock. Sometimes they'd go to the Peabody Museum and identify their pieces, hanging over the show-cases together for hours. Sandy had taken her to school dances a couple of times, too—he was a nice kid.

But not so nice as Hank Sutton. Nobody could be as nice as Hank. The girls couldn't tease her about him, because he was her foster-cousin. Hank and Sally were only a year apart. When Wincy came they made a threesome. Some-times they went to the early movie in the Square; sometimes they went to chamber-music concerts in Hank's House at Harvard. They often had brother-sister scraps and Sally would lose her temper. But she really adored Hank, and when he left for the army, Sally said it was the end of all good times. In a way it had been.

Hank was tall and well built, just like Uncle Harley, with the same large, clever hands and black hair that stood up from his head like a brush. It was funny to see them together— they looked so much alike.

Wincy loved Uncle Harley. How wonderful it was when you were ill to have him come running over, toting his instrument bag. You felt better the minute he arrived—he had such a kind, quiet way of looking at you. Angus had been very proud when he had to have his appendix out. He had the idea Uncle Harley only operated on professors, so for weeks after he was well, Angus went around boasting to everyone that Doctor Sutton had operated on *him*.

When they first arrrived, and Angus saw Uncle Bill playing catch with Sutty after supper, or making things with him down in the workshop, he became furiously jealous of Sutty.

Of course he didn't say anything. He just wet his bed. Wincy herself wouldn't have understood if Uncle Bill hadn't explained about the subconscious, and all those different layers in your mind. Uncle Bill was wonderful the way he made you see things—no wonder he was so popular with the students. Hank said just about everybody at Harvard wanted to take Uncle Bill's chem courses.

Even Sutty had been swell to Angus. He was eight when they arrived, and Angus was only five, but Sutty dragged him around with his gang, introducing him to everyone as "my kid brother." If Mummie knew some of the scrapes Angus had been in with Sutty. . . .

Pretty soon Angus began to feel Uncle Bill cared for him, that he treated him just like Sutty. After that first camping trip the three of them took, Angus never wet again, until the night before they sailed.

Aunt Polly had said a lot of nice things to Wincy that night. She also reminded her that different countries had different customs and that it was a mistake to make comparisons. Wincy must try to adjust to Oxford as she had to Belmont.

It was impossible to believe now that Wincy had ever had trouble adjusting to life in Belmont. Living there had been as natural as breathing. And yet, Wincy remembered that the first year, she had often been blue and that she probably taxed Aunt Polly's patience quite a bit. Very soon, though, she saw how lucky she and Angus had been falling in with the Hilliards, especially when she went to visit Evelyn Derby in the elegant house on Beacon Street where she had been given a home.

Evelyn had been taken in by nice, middle-aged people who had been so distressed by the bombing of England that they eagerly opened their home to a little refugee. The only thing Wincy didn't like about them was the embarrassing way they made Evelyn speak before their friends in order to show off her British accent. They thought it "cute."

And yet, in a way, they were hostile to it, too, for they insisted on pronouncing her name "Evvulyn Derby,"—the American way—instead of "Eevlyn Darby," which was the proper way. That made Evelyn positively livid.

Her foster-parents meant well, for they showered expensive presents on Evelyn, sent her to private school, and went out of their way to make her happy. But before she had time to find out what it was all about, they expected her to do things like an American girl her age.

The first week she was in Boston, Evelyn was rushed to the beauty-parlour for a permanent. She hadn't wanted it, of course, and Wincy could sympathize with that. She herself hadn't wanted a permanent until after she had been in America three years. But the very week she arrived, Evelyn had to have her hair frizzed and get a long taffeta dress and high-heeled slippers, and instead of being grateful for all these luxuries, Evelyn told her foster-mother frankly that she thought she looked "ghahstly."

Though much too young, Evelyn was taken to the Junior Cotillion and faithfully escorted to every new movie that came to town, but Evelyn, fresh from a parsonage-nursery in Somerset, confided to Wincy that the only thing she really cared for in Boston was going to the Public Gardens and riding on the swanboats.

Gradually a stubborn streak that had not been there before developed in Evelyn, making her seem even more British than she had been at home. She went about comparing everything in Boston unfavourably with both London and Somerset, running down the school her foster-parents were paying for, and making herself—and through herself, her country— thoroughly disliked.

Wincy was sorry, but she didn't blame Evelyn. She might have acted that way herself, if the Hilliards had rushed her into adopting their ways. But of course the Hilliards never did anything like that. They were too sensible.

After a couple of years, Evelyn's foster-parents decided she was hopelessly unresponsive. America was in the war by then. Evelyn's foster-mother lost her cook and became a nurse's aide. Since the danger of invasion seemed definitely past for England, and it couldn't be said that Evelyn was getting along swimmingly in Beacon Street, there seemed no point in continuing the relationship, and she was shipped back to Somerset.

Poor Evelyn, Wincy thought. She was nice, and so were her foster-parents. It was just one of those situations—life was an awful puzzle, sometimes. Now, what was the matter with calling your own brother a bum, she wondered. It's slang, she thought, but quite polite, really. Wincy could think of worse words.

Remembering about Belmont, after the miserable afternoon, had been like swallowing warm milk and honey when she had a sore throat. It took the ache away and left her mind all peaceful.

She must have been asleep, for the next thing she knew, she was wakened by a little scraping sound. The door opened a crack and Wincy half expected to see Brindle, Sutty's pup, pushing in his snout. But it was Angus, carrying a tray of cocoa and biscuits.

"Mummie sent you this supper," he said, looking sorrowfully at Wincy. "I'm sorry I swiped the crumpet."

"I don't want supper," Wincy said. "Never mind about the crumpet. It wasn't your fault I said something so world shaking. Here I am, all grown up, and they're trying to make an infant of me again, sending me to my room."

Angus sat down on the edge of her bed resting his yellow

head sideways on his knees and looking so sad that Wincy almost smiled. Gosh, he was a good kid.

"Wincy," he said, when he had thought a while, "let's go back. It's rotten here."

She reached out and stroked his stubbly hair. "We can't, goofy," she said.

"Gosh," he sighed, "I didn't think English people were going to be like that."

"It might be just Mummie and Daddy," Wincy said, as much to herself as to Angus. "After all, when it comes to handling kids, they're just beginners."

"Yes," Angus agreed, sighing again. "Got to give them time, I guess."

"If only I knew what I'd done," Wincy complained wearily. "Maybe if Mark was here, he'd tell me. I wish he was. If I only knew—"

"I know," Angus said, sitting up suddenly. "Francis told me in the passage. He thought it was a big joke."

"What? What's a big joke?"

"Bum doesn't mean the same thing here it does at home," Angus explained.

"Oh," said Wincy, sitting up suddenly, too.

"That's why they got so mad," Angus continued.

"But I wonder what it does mean," Wincy said, trying to remember whether she had ever heard the word in nursery days. "I wish he'd told you that."

"He did," said Angus. "It means fanny."

VII

ANGUS WAS in the doghouse, too. He came in the next morning to tell Wincy about it.

The night before, Mrs. Turner had insisted that in addition to his pyjamas, Angus wear a flannel band around his tummy. Angus had refused. His mother had insisted. Wincy knew there was no use insisting when Angus refused and there was no use refusing when her mother insisted—they were alike that way.

It wasn't clear to her how things had come out, but Wincy had heard the mattress being heaved down the stairs.

Mrs. Turner, however, didn't notice it until much later, when she was gathering acorns. She was sitting with her legs stretched straight out before her on a root of the great oak at the bottom of the garden. She wore her bottle-green W.V.S. uniform and a matching hat with the brim turned down in front and up in back, almost, Wincy thought, like the ones the boys and girls at Agassiz used to wear after the whole class had autographed them.

"For Pete's sake, Mummie," Angus shouted, as he and Wincy came out, "what the heck do you think you're doing?"

"W.V.S.," his mother answered, intent on her job of collecting.

"But what do they want acorns for?" Angus asked, in a tone of bewilderment.

"Pigs—the pigs of Oxfordshire," Mrs. Turner explained, looking up.

It was then that she saw the mattress. She was quite upset.

She didn't exactly scold Angus, but from the way she talked, Wincy thought, she must believe it was nothing but naughtiness that made him wet.

"You oughtn't to be angry with him, Mummie," Wincy broke in, "it'll only make matters worse. He'd stop wetting, I'm sure, if you could only make him feel you love him. That worked in Belmont."

Her mother turned on Wincy. "Do stop talking nonsense, child," she commanded. "You're merely putting ideas into his head, very unhealthy, and improper ideas, which you picked up in America. I've noticed you have a good many of them."

Wincy thought her mother was going to cry.

"How can you talk about my loving him? Every mother loves her children. You can't think how I suffered while you were gone. And now to have you tell me I don't love my own boy."

"I only said if you could make him *feel* you love him," Wincy said softly.

"English people of good taste do not display their emotions," Mrs. Turner said. Having settled the argument, she left the garden.

This isn't getting Angus anywhere, Wincy thought. I wonder whether Daddy understands—someone has to help Angus.

Professor Turner's study was a little room at the back of the house, rather a poor place for work, Wincy thought, because it was very dark. She knocked on the door and looked in.

"Do you mind, Daddy?"

Her father looked up from the papers on his desk.

"Not this once," he said, "if you have something of importance to say. But Angus makes a practice of popping in at all times and what he has to tell me is of little consequence. He even follows me into my dressing-room—no sense of privacy."

"I suppose not," Wincy said. "We ran all over the Hilliards' house. Nobody minded. I guess Angus follows you around because he's lonely."

Professor Turner looked at his watch.

"What was it you came to see me about, chicken?" he asked. "What with the vegetable-garden and fire-watching, I have all too little time for my book. Sit over there, where I can see you."

"It's about Angus wetting his bed."

Embarrassment was so plainly marked in her father's face that Wincy stopped. She wondered what could possibly have caused it—surely nothing to do with Angus's wetting. Uncle Bill had talked it over with her loads of times. Then she thought the most polite thing would be not to notice his embarrassment, so she went on.

"It's no good scolding Angus for wetting," she explained. "You could cure him, just the way Uncle Bill did."

"I?" Professor Turner asked in astonishment, and Wincy saw that little beads of perspiration were forming on his nose. "How could I possibly? This is a case for a kidney specialist. Your mother ought to consult one."

"No, Daddy, it's not."

"In any case," Professor Turner concluded, "it is not a matter for a father to discuss with his young daughter."

Wincy pulled at her father's sleeve.

"Look, Daddy, let me tell you about it. Angus and I felt

terribly unhappy those first weeks at the Hilliards', when he wet—we were so anxious to make a good impression. But we needn't have worried, because Aunt Polly didn't fuss at all. She just showed Angus how to work the pulley line."

Professor Turner looked puzzled.

"Skip it," Wincy said. "That's not the point. It's just a contraption the Hilliards have for hanging out the washing."

"I see."

"Angus felt frightened," Wincy continued, "because everything was strange and he didn't have Nannie."

"We feared that would be the case when you left," Professor Turner said, and now he looked quite calm again. "But under the circumstances, with invasion threatening us any day—"

"Certainly," Wincy said. There was no use going into that. "The main trouble, though, was that Angus was jealous of Sutty Hilliard. You see, when Uncle Bill comes home in the evening, he does things with Sutty. They work the electric trains or make airplane models and water-wheels. In the summer they play catch in the back yard."

"Indeed?" Professor Turner asked with surprise.

"Angus had never had fun like that with you," Wincy went on. "When he was brought down to the drawing room after tea, you thought him so noisy that Mummie would ring for Nannie to take him away again. And you seldom went to the nursery."

"No," he agreed. "Nannie didn't seem to like it."

"Seeing Sutty and Uncle Bill chummy together made Angus jealous."

Her father gave Wincy a searching look.

"Tell me, my dear, in Belmont—in the States—do fathers

make a practice of spending their leisure in the nursery?"

"They don't really have nurseries," Wincy answered. "Families just do things together."

"Indeed—"

"When Angus got to feel that Uncle Bill cared for him, as well as for Sutty, he stopped wetting. Uncle Bill let the boys help him paint and fix things. The three of them made a crystal set. They had a lot of fun. A couple of weeks after we got there, they went on a little camping trip. After that, Angus stopped wetting."

Professor Turner looked puzzled. "I cannot see the relation between this—this ailment of Angus's and a camping trip," he said. "I should have thought, on the contrary, that exposure and dampness would only serve to aggravate the condition."

"It's psychology—don't you see?" Wincy leaned forward in the chair. "This isn't an illness," she said earnestly. "Something in his mind bothers Angus while he sleeps and makes him wet. I think he wants to be chums with you, the way Sutty is with his father."

Professor Turner's face lit up with a sudden flash of understanding. "You mean, if I were more—more companionable? Would that really make a difference?" he asked. "But I don't know how to make water-wheels and airplanes. I haven't a notion how 'catch' is played. And nowadays my time is taken up with teaching and fire-watching, Home Guarding and home gardening." He looked up to see whether Wincy caught the joke.

"I know," Wincy said, smiling.

"In any case," her father continued, "I'm too old. When I was a boy, I was obliged to study such long hours in order to win exhibitions that I had no time for childish games."

"Poor little kid," Wincy murmured.

"Then," the Professor went on, without noticing her comment, "I had to work even harder for the University scholarships, and finally, the Fellowship which I held at St. James's until my marriage to your mother. This Fellowship prevented me from marrying until late in life. I am fifty-eight, you know. In point of age, I could be Angus's grandfather."

"Yes, that does make a difference," Wincy reflected. "Uncle Bill is only thirty-eight and Sutty is already twelve."

"Yet," Professor Turner continued thoughtfully, "I was no closer to Mark, when he was a lad. But I never thought he needed me."

"Oh, Daddy, he must have."

"No, I never thought he did. First he had Nannie, and when he was nine he went to St. Tim's. In the holidays he was always busy with rugger and other boyish pursuits. And yet, there may be something to what you say about companionship. I wish now that I had known him more intimately— the thought occurred to me the day he left to join his squadron. I would have more to remember him by than just his outward appearance, if we had done things together. But, of course, I could never have devoted much time to him."

"Oh, Daddy, you do understand! Please try to help Angus. He needs you."

Wincy felt happy. She had managed to get her idea across.

"I shall," her father said. "Some day we'll read the classics together, Angus and I."

Well, did he understand? She had thought so at first, but now Wincy wondered.

Her father was looking at her curiously. "You're very

knowledgeable, Wincy," he said. "How do you come to see things with the wisdom of a grown woman at the age of fifteen?"

Wincy was pleased. Her father was beginning to think of her as an adult.

"Aunt Polly and Uncle Bill explained psychology to me so I could help Angus," she said. "He began wetting again the night before we sailed for home. And then, on the boat, that rotten stewardess—"

"Psychology," Professor Turner repeated, wrinkling his forehead.

"Yes," said Wincy, "Uncle Bill and Aunt Polly know quite a lot about it. Ever since they were in college, they've been studying behaviour."

"Behaviour does not strike me as a fitting subject for university study," Professor Turner remarked irritably. "Here in England most of us learned to behave when we were in the nursery."

A suspicion began to grow in Wincy's mind. Perhaps psychology was one of those strictly American things—like corn on the cob and baseball and sweet potatoes—that are unknown in England.

Professor Turner was rubbing his eyes. They looked very tired.

"The light is poor in here," Wincy said.

"Yes," her father agreed, "the wistaria has grown out of hand. It wants trimming, but we've not been able to get a gardener."

"Angus will do it," Wincy said. "He and Sutty did all the gardening at the Hilliards'."

Professor Turner looked up in surprise. "Do you suppose

a little chap like that could?" he asked. "It would help a great deal. I didn't mind so long as the student-lamp was functioning, but I haven't been able to use it for a year. All of a sudden one day there was a spurt of electric current. It gave me quite a turn."

"Did the fuse blow out?"

"I can't say. I have thrice asked Purseglove to send a man, but none has come. In former times Purseglove was always so reliable. He doesn't have anyone to send now, I expect. And my reading-stand wants mending, but the joiner—" his voice trailed off despondently.

Wincy looked at the lamp-cord. The silk was frayed around the plug, exposing the wires.

"Angus can probably fix it," she said.

This time her father thought Wincy was joking. He laughed.

"I mean it," Wincy insisted. "He's quite good at things like that. Angus and Sutty made hundreds of lamps and thingumajigs. You should have seen their silly telephone."

"Do you mean the Hilliards'?"

"No, no—the one Sutty and Angus rigged up between their rooms. To be heard at all through it, they had to shout so loud that their voices carried across the hall, even with the doors shut."

"They might just as well have opened the doors and eliminated the telephone altogether, mightn't they?" Professor Turner asked.

"Yes," said Wincy, patiently. "But it was fun to rig up."

"I see."

Wincy put her arms around her father, wondering what he could have been like when he was a little boy

"I'll get Angus to fix the lamp right now," she said, kissing the top of his silver head. "But I think it would be nice if you asked him to do the vine—as between men, you know," she added, laughing.

Wincy found Angus sitting on the kitchen step, bouncing his football.

"Gosh, there's nothing to do here," he complained.

"Yes, there is. Daddy needs you."

"Who—me? He just told me to scram."

"Well, he needs you now."

"He *does*?"

Angus jumped up and raced to his father's study, followed by Wincy.

"It will be a great boon to me if you can put the student-lamp to rights, my boy," Professor Turner said gravely. " 'This whole house is plunged in ruin . . .' as Euripides puts it in the *Medea*."

"Sure I will," Angus replied, examining the plug. "All I need is a screw-driver. Where is it? I'll get it."

"A screw-driver?" Professor Turner repeated. "I've never seen one, but there's doubtless something of the sort in the house."

"Gosh," Angus said, "in the Hilliards' workshop there were—" but Wincy had caught his eye and he stopped.

Angus hunted in the scullery and finally returned with an implement equal to the job. He sat on the floor of the study, opened the plug and put the loosened wire back inside.

Wincy saw the admiration with which her father recognized his little boy's skill. She went quietly out of the room so that the new companions could feel free to talk. But she lingered at the door.

"You put me in mind of Prometheus, my boy," she heard her father say. "You are bringing me light."

There was a long silence.

"When I was your age," Professor Turner continued, "I could recite whole passages of *Prometheus*."

There was another silence. Then Wincy heard Angus's voice. "I wonder what's happening to Joe Palooka," he said dreamily.

"Was he one of your New England playfellows?"

"No."

"Who then, my boy?" Professor Turner asked.

There was another silence.

"Aw," Angus said, finally, with a sigh of despair, "you wouldn't know."

VIII

"It's Mark," Wincy thought, seeing a tall, lean figure through the glass panel as she came downstairs. That's how he looked—his hair parted on the side, wearing a cricket-blazer . . . Mark!

She ran to open the door, rumpling the rug in her haste.

It wasn't Mark, though, just Francis Quelch with a Latin book he had borrowed.

What must he think of her, after the break she made yesterday?

Wincy wanted to run upstairs, but it was too late—he had already seen her. Well, Francis shouldn't think she minded what had happened. She tried to look lofty and bored, like a model in *Vogue*.

"I say," Francis began, smiling at her as though nothing had happened, "will you please give this to Professor Turner?"

"Certainly," Wincy drawled languidly, lifting her nose so high that she could feel the skin stretch along her throat.

Now that he had delivered the book, there was nothing further to detain him. Wincy did wish he would go. Her neck was getting very tired.

Francis didn't stir. He just stood there, looking at Wincy in a nice, smiling sort of way, a little puzzled, but friendly.

She tried to look still more bored.

"Beautiful day," he remarked.

"Extremely," Wincy agreed.

It was getting so she could hardly swallow.

Francis shifted his weight from one foot to another, smiled at Wincy, looked at the ceiling, and smiled at her again.

"Well," he said at last, "I thought I'd just pop in with the book. Cheerio!"

Really, it was about time—

Still looking at her in that funny way, Francis made for the door and tripped over the hump in the rug.

"Oh," he cried in alarm. "I thought I'd trod on the dog."

Somehow, it struck her so funny, Wincy couldn't help laughing. And then Francis laughed.

"We don't have Duffy any more," Wincy explained. "I remember, you used to pull his tail."

"Did I?"

"Yes, and my braids."

"Did I? You make me sound an awful rotter. I expect I pulled your leg, as well. I say, I *am* sorry."

They laughed again.

All at once, Wincy noticed that her chin was at its usual level. It didn't matter now. Francis seemed to have forgotten the break she had made. Besides, from all accounts, he had his troubles, too.

"Is the Latin bad?" Wincy asked.

"Candidly, it's most frightful," he answered. "I swot all day—there are such hundreds of pages. I've only a month till Smalls, and the River's ever so jolly now."

"Smalls?" That was a new word for her.

"Responsions, you know," Francis explained. "Examinations to let me into the University."

"What if you flunk?" Wincy asked, and immediately regretted being a kill-joy.

"Flunk?" That must be a new word for him.

"Don't pass."

"Oh, I see. You mean batted. I should be very pleased, actually. I'm bound to say, I don't really want to go up. It's Father's plan. I want to join the Navy. But Father's pig headed."

Wincy looked up into his face earnestly. "The older generation doesn't understand a lot of things," she said sympathetically, thinking of her own parents.

He nodded, but his forehead wrinkled up. "D'you know, Wincy," he said slowly, "it's impossible to believe you're not much older than Brenda?"

She really wasn't any older—five days younger, as a matter of fact—but she was too polite to say so. She didn't want to hurt Francis by agreeing that his sister was a baby.

"I expect America was an eye-opener—everything so large and wonderful," he said. "Did you ever go to New York?"

"Yes, Aunt Polly took us there once in vacation," Wincy answered, glowing. This was the first time anyone in Oxford had asked about her travels. "We saw the Planetarium and ate at the Automat and went to the top of the Empire State Building. It was wonderful."

Francis looked impressed. "Sounds jolly," he exclaimed.

Wincy suddenly decided to ask him the question that had come to her when she was talking to her father about Angus.

"Francis," she began, and then stopped. Suppose he laughed at her?

But he was looking down at her inquiringly, and there was something so straightforward in his face that Wincy felt certain she could ask him.

"Francis, do English people know about psychology—inferiority complexes and that sort of thing?"

He thought for a long time. "Candidly, not very much. I believe they're doing some experiments in Cambridge—"

"What about Oxford?" Wincy asked, so eagerly that she cut him short.

"Oh, not at Oxford. At least," he added, doubtfully, "I shouldn't think so. Never any new ideas at St. James's, at least. Just the old traditional studies—might as well be back in the Middle Ages, monks and all, don't you think?" And he laughed.

So that was it—that explained everything. Her parents just hadn't heard about psychology—back in the Middle Ages. You couldn't blame them, then, for not understanding. And she sighed, thinking of all the things she would have to teach them.

"Thumbs up!" said Francis. "You sound melancholy. I

expect it's a bit of a tax for you, coming back to Merrie England."

"Oh, not for me," Wincy assured him. "Just for Angus. Do you go out on the River often?"

"Whenever I can. I was on my way now, as a matter of fact."

"Oh," said Wincy.

There was a little silence. Francis didn't seem to know how to leave. American boys were like that, too.

"I say," he said suddenly, his face brightening, "would you like to come along?"

"I'd love to," Wincy said.

"Cheers!" cried Francis. "But I mean—what I want to say is—well—do you think your mother will allow it?"

Wincy looked at him with pity.

"Does Brenda have to ask permission to go out in the day-time? Well, of course, it's different here. I don't have to ask any more. American girls our age needn't, just so we get home in time to help with dinner." She looked at him earnestly. "We will be home in time, won't we? I'd hate to let Mummie down."

"We'll be back on the tick," Francis assured her. "Matter of fact, I'll have to swot a bit this afternoon or Father will be after me."

"Let's go," said Wincy gaily, opening the door.

This was going to be fun. This was like being back in Cambridge and going out with Sandy Whipple or Hank Sutton.

They walked together down the path to the garden-gate. As Wincy passed through it, she took a deep breath. Since the night she arrived, she hadn't been beyond the garden. It had been dark then, and in her impatience to see home, she hadn't noticed anything else.

Now she looked up and down Banbury Road at the rows of brick houses hiding modestly behind their walls. Suddenly she was covered by a shower of laburnum petals coming out of the neighbouring garden. It blew against her face like golden rain.

"Oh," Wincy exclaimed in her surprise, "how lovely Oxford is!"

Francis was standing still by the gate.

"Which way do we go?" she asked him.

He didn't answer, but stood there, looking troubled.

"Look here, Wincy," he said at last, "hadn't you better tell your mother that you're going?"

"It's not at all necessary," she assured him. Then she added, just to be a sport, "But if you'd rather, I will."

She looked up, and seeing that was what he wished, she went back.

Mrs. Turner was up in the nursery looking through Angus's clothing and counting her coupons. "There you are," she said, as Wincy came in. "I couldn't think where you were keeping yourself all this time. I've not a very great deal of coupons."

Wincy had no time to discuss this now. Standing near the window, she could see Francis waiting for her in the street. "I'm going on the River with Francis," she told her mother.

Mrs. Turner looked up and blinked at Wincy, as if, concentrating on her calculation, she had not quite heard.

"I'm going on the River with Francis," Wincy repeated, and bent over to kiss her mother good-bye.

"You'll not do anything of the sort, my dear." Her mother was firm.

"But I've told him I would go," Wincy insisted. "I'll be back in time to help get dinner."

"You are going shopping with me," Mrs. Turner said calmly. "I think we have enough coupons to get a frock for you *or* an Oxford grey suit for Angus. He can't possibly wear his American clothes to the Warden's garden party. Yet you do need a frock. I don't know which to choose."

"Oh, Mummie, you didn't tell me you were planning to take me shopping," Wincy cried. "If I'd known, I wouldn't have made the date with Francis."

"You should have asked permission first in any case, my love. You're far too young," Mrs. Turner said, smiling indulgently at Wincy.

"What'll I do?" Wincy asked desperately, looking to her mother for help. "I can't stand Francis up. In our crowd a girl who would stand a boy up was—"

"There is no question as to what you will do," Mrs. Turner said, putting her coupons away. "You are coming with me."

Wincy knew there was nothing to do but to explain to Francis. Angry and embarrassed, she hurried across the straggling landing and down the two flights of stairs. It seemed, as she crossed the passage, that she heard her mother call. She stood still a moment to listen, but the house was quiet.

From the door only a few feet of the street beyond the garden-gate were visible: the rest was hidden by the wall. Although she couldn't see Francis, Wincy knew that he was waiting for her. "Cheers!" That was what he had exclaimed when she said she would go with him.

She hurried down the path and through the gate.

Francis wasn't there. He was half-way up the street, disappearing very rapidly. He never stopped to look back.

Wincy bit her lip, but her eyes would prickle. So he was a drip, after all. . . . She turned slowly and dragged herself back toward the house.

Lifting her head, she noticed through the tears that Mrs. Turner was standing at the nursery-window.

All at once, Wincy understood what had happened. Her mother had called to Francis from the window, just as she would have done years ago, when they were still kids. Her mother had sent him away.

IX

WINCY WAS relieved to be out of doors. Her fury had died down—Aunt Polly hated people who griped—but every time she thought about the way her mother had sent Francis off, she felt hot and stifled. It was better outside. Once again she was surprised to see how lovely everything was, just as she had felt a few hours before, when she stood at the garden-gate with Francis and the laburnum covered her with a shower of golden petals.

As she and Angus walked down Banbury Road with Mrs. Turner, she began to feel smoothed out inside. Why had she never thought more about the streets of Oxford while she was away? They were so lovely, with the maytrees and chestnut candles in full bloom and climbing roses dropping over the garden-walls.

Whenever she did think of home—and she had not thought

of it very much during her last two years away—it was always indoors that she pictured, usually the nursery. And yet, Nannie had taken them walking every day. But Nannie had dreaded the traffic in Carfax and the crowds in the Cornmarket, so she confined the route to Woodstock Road and the Parks where she could be certain of meeting other nurses. It was deadly dull, Wincy thought.

"I fear I shan't be able to get you a frock and Angus a knicker-suit as well," Mrs. Turner said. "The coupons, you know. But Mrs. Tippet may be able to contrive something for you out of my old Liberty print. Mrs. Tippet is an excellent needle-woman."

"Not a smock, *please*, Mummie. I've plenty of clothes— really I have." Wincy insisted. "Beautiful ones."

"They are nice," Mrs. Turner acknowledged, in the tone one uses to soothe a child. "You may wear them at home, and for certain occasions. But for the Warden's garden party you will need something more appropriate. I do wish I could buy you a pretty frock, my love, but I fear Angus needs the suit more."

"Yes, get Angus the suit."

"I fear I must. He cannot wear that American outfit to the Warden's. It does seem a pity, though, to spend coupons on shorts, for he'll want trousers in September, when he goes away to school."

"Goes away to school? Mummie, you're not thinking of sending Angus away?—to *boarding-school*?"

"Why not? He's nine," Mrs. Turner said placidly.

Wincy looked around quickly to see if Angus had heard. This was awful—worse, even, than the way her mother had acted about Francis.

But Angus was half-way down the street, squeezing under railings and balancing on top of garden-walls. His mother looked around bewildered, trying to keep track of his rapid movements, yet too preoccupied with planning her shopping to call him back.

"There's one thing we can get for you, though," she said brightly, "—a new hat."

Wincy groaned to herself.

Oh, what's the diff, she thought bitterly, if only they don't send Angus away . . . I don't mind half so much what they do to me. He knows how to take care of himself now, but still—

Going over on that crowded boat, Angus had had a dreadful time with his shoes. Nannie had always said that since Angus either tied a bow that would immediately open, or else a knot that would never come undone, she preferred to lace them herself.

Angus had run around the deck with his laces flapping until he tripped. Then he sat down on the wet planks—what would Nannie have said?—and tugged, tugged till the laces broke. He had bellowed for a new pair, just as he would have done at home. Angus's bellowing was *something* in those days, but none of the people in charge had time to listen to him. At last, one of the little deckhands showed him how to tie the broken ends together and hide the knot inside the shoe. Angus was tremendously pleased with the new discovery.

On the return journey, there had been that stewardess, who made unkind and quite unnecessary remarks about his mattress. Now he was to go away again, alone. There must be a way to stop it.

"He's much too young," Wincy said. It was the first objection she could think of.

"Angus—you mean? I thought we were discussing hats," Mrs. Turner said gaily. "Not really young—though he seems so, I grant you. But Mark went away when he was nine. Many boys do."

"Mark spent such hours packing his tuck box," Wincy recalled. "And Cook used to fume for fear the cake and jam-roll she had baked for him would get squashed by his toys."

Her mother turned to Wincy with a look of pleasure. "Do you remember? How lovely! You never mention Mark—I feared you, like Angus, had quite forgotten him."

"I remember the tuck box," Wincy answered. "Mark was always cross for fear I'd touch it."

Mrs. Turner laughed. "Good old Mark—" she said lovingly. "He did guard it vigilantly—I remember how he clung to it his first term, not wanting the porter to take it to the luggage-van. I'm afraid he was more concerned about his tuck box than he was about leaving home. He stood there at the railway-station amongst the old boys, who wouldn't make friends with him, looking so forlorn, poor little chap."

"And you want to send Angus—oh, Mummie, how cruel!"

"Mark came to love St. Timothy's, after the first few terms. I wish he were there yet," she put in wistfully. "Those were such safe, happy days." Her thought shifted to Angus. "He'll get excellent preparation for Winchester and make nice friends—it'll be jolly for him. From time to time," she added, to cheer Wincy, "we'll send him a hamper."

"Couldn't he prepare for Winchester in Oxford?" Wincy pleaded. "What about St. George's School?"

"Angus is going there next week for the remainder of

term. The classics master is going to give him special help. I can't think why the school the Hilliards chose for him didn't teach Latin."

"Nobody takes Latin in grammar-school in America," Wincy said.

"How strange—for a boy. At all events," Mrs. Turner said with finality, "Angus will go to St. Tim's in September. Perhaps if we had a governess—"

"A governess, Mummie! Angus would be too old for one. You don't seem to realize what it was like in Belmont. He used to—" Wincy stopped. Her mother's expression warned her that this line of reasoning was not politic.

"And then there is his habit of—of wetting." Mrs. Turner went on quickly. "He will soon overcome it at boarding-school. The other boys will tease him out of it."

Wincy went suddenly sick inside. She could see Angus standing in a dormitory with his wet sheets, surrounded by a crowd of jeering little boys. That would certainly give him some kind of a complex.

"Do you *want* them to tease him?" she asked incredulously.

"Of course not, dear," Mrs. Turner said. "Still, it might cure him. . . ."

It was like a trap, Wincy thought, this lack of understanding on her mother's part. "Daddy told me yesterday that he'd give more time to Angus when the vac begins," she said desperately. "Take him walks and things. That will cure him, I'm sure."

"Dear man—" Mrs. Turner said, smiling indulgently, "it's good of him to want to relieve me of the child occasionally. But John hardly takes the place of a governess. If only I could put my hands on one. . . . Besides, with Home Guard

and fire-watching and his garden, your father's overworked
as it is. And he's rather nervy just at present anyhow—something to do with St. James's."

"I know, Mummie. What's it about?"

"A very grown-up sort of thing, my dear—nothing to
bother your little head over at all."

They had reached St. John's College and the Martyrs'
Memorial. Wincy used to shiver when she walked past here,
not daring to read the inscription, and yet not being able to
resist looking at the words . . . "who near this spot yielded
their bodies to be burned . . ." Even now, Wincy remembered that Bishop Cranmer had put his right hand in the flame
first because it had signed his recantation. She sighed as she
walked by.

Magdalen Street and the Cornmarket were more crowded
than Wincy had expected. Boys and girls in uniform and
undergraduates with ragged little gowns hanging from their
shoulders overflowed the pavement.

Wincy noticed that many of the ladies looked at her legs.
She began to feel embarrassed. Mrs. Turner noticed it, too.

"They're admiring your American stockings," she said.
"No one in England has any like that."

Angus was sticking close to his mother now. "It's like
Tremont Street," he said.

"Evacuees," Mrs. Turner explained. "Down from Town."

"They ought to go home," Angus said. "We had to."

"Not 'had to', Angus," Wincy whispered hastily. She
guessed, from watching her mother's serene expression, that
she had not noticed the slip.

"Look," Angus said, "there's an American flag—isn't that
nice?"

"Need you shout so, dear? It's the old Clarendon Hotel," Mrs. Turner explained. "They've converted it into an American Red Cross Club."

As she spoke, she shepherded the children into a long department store.

"Oh, I remember," Wincy said, "we used to buy my gym tunics here and those awful beaver hats."

"Right you are!" her mother answered, leading the way to a part of the store marked Boys' and Girls' Complete School Outfits. "A summer hat for Newfields School, please," she said to the assistant.

Before Wincy could think what was going to happen, there it was on her head, the very same straw model she used to wear before she went away, with the blue-and-gold Newfields band around the crown.

"But I'm not going to school," Wincy told the shop-assistant crossly.

"Of course not, Wincy," her mother put in sharply. "Don't be sticky. I just thought, since we have to be so careful with our coupons, that you might as well get a school hat now. You'll need it when you do go."

The clerk put a mirror into Wincy's hand. It was not exactly an unbecoming hat—rather Peck and Peckish or Dobbs. But so young . . .

"Keep it on," Mrs. Turner said briskly, as she parted with the coupons. "I should like to see you wear it home." And Wincy knew that the matter was settled before she had had a chance to fight . . . like Czecho-Slovakia at Munich, she thought.

Angus was less easily fitted. It was not a question of choice, for nearly all the suits were Oxford grey, and Mrs. Turner, feeling the cloth between her thumb and forefinger, declared them all shoddy. But Angus was too big for a knicker-suit.

"Only nine years old!" the old man who measured him marvelled. "What a great young gentleman."

"It's all that milk I drank in America," Angus explained proudly, expanding his chest.

At last they found one that would do for the next few months.

"Wear it home," Mrs. Turner urged. "You look ever so much nicer. I'll take the old garments." She held out her market-basket.

They came out of the shop again, Angus, except for his crew-cut, looking quite English, and Wincy much more so.

A little farther down the street, Angus stopped suddenly and clutched Wincy's arm.

"Wincy, Wincy, look—Woolworth's!" he shouted. "Just like the five-and-ten in Brattle Square, only the paint's wore off. Let's go in."

Mrs. Turner hesitated. Nannie had never approved of taking children into crowded shops. Wincy had been taken only when necessary—if she had to be fitted at the bootmakers in the High, or measured for her riding-habit.

"Very well," Mrs. Turner consented at length, going in. "It can't hurt—just for a few moments. I need some shoe-blacking." She went off to find it.

"Smells just like the five-and-ten in Cambridge," Angus said happily. "Peoply."

Wincy wrinkled her nose. "What do you want?"

"A scratch-pad."

They went to the stationery counter. There was not much on sale.

"A scratch-pad, please," Angus said to the clerk.

She looked at him blankly. "What sort of thing do you wish to scratch?"

Angus leaned across the high counter and pointed to what he wanted. He could not quite reach it.

"Oo," the girl exclaimed. "You mean a scribbly-block. What ever could you scratch with it? Sixpence."

"Gosh," Angus said to Wincy in astonishment. "It wouldn't cost more than a nickel at home."

"Any pencils?" the girl was asking.

Angus nodded.

"Afraid I haven't any rubbers," she said contritely.

"That's okay," Angus assured her. "I have a pair."

"Oo, what a lucky duck. Some people use a wad of bread. Smudges, though."

Angus moved closer to Wincy. "Guess she's nuts," he whispered, nodding toward the clerk.

Wincy was picking out postcards to send to her friends at Agassiz. She owed it to her father to get pictures of St. James's College, but she did think Christ Church, with its beautiful Tom Tower, much nicer.

She and Angus were having a lovely time just mooning about when their mother came up and hurried them out of the store. She explained that she was eager to stop at Mrs. Tippet's on the way home, else Wincy's frock would not be done by May Day.

"What's May Day?" Angus asked.

"The Warden's garden party," Mrs. Turner explained. "It used to be quite a posh affair in peacetime. Now it's merely a quiet gathering of Fellows and their families—not really a party at all. Nevertheless, we want to appear our best."

She looked very pleased and proud as she walked back up Magdalen Street with a fairly civilized-looking child on either side.

But as soon as they were out of the crowd again, Angus began straying. He tried standing on the water-table that runs along the west front of Balliol College. It was not a simple thing to do. He tried St. John's, evidently hoping that that would be easier, but it wasn't.

"Bless me—" Mrs. Turner exclaimed, as Angus suddenly fell flat on his stomach in the middle of the pavement.

It was clear, even before his mother caught up with him, that he was not hurt, for there was an expression of great satisfaction on his face.

"Got him!" he announced triumphantly, as his mother rushed up.

"Got whom?" She stood over him, shocked.

"Commandoes," Angus explained cryptically.

"What are you talking about? Do get up at once, Angus. Just see how dusty you've got your new suit. And your hands are black."

"Have to be," Angus replied gruffly, rubbing the dirt into his suit in a misguided attempt to brush it off. "Faces too. It's so we won't be caught."

"Fancy throwing yourself in the mud in your new suit. . . ." Mrs. Turner cried wearily. She did not seem cross with Angus so much as with life, for giving her such a trying job.

Mrs. Turner rode beautifully. Why couldn't her job have been something to do with horses? She was also very clever at training dogs and she could spout yards and yards from the Bible. She was considered one of the ablest workers in the W.V.S., darning socks for what seemed like whole regiments, decorating Army hostels with flowers and chintzes, and gathering feed for sties full of pigs. She was very good at all these things. But kid commandoes . . .

They walked on in uncomfortable silence.

May

X

AFTER THE first minute, when she recovered from the surprise, Wincy stood back and looked at Hank. She hadn't remembered he was so handsome, but then, she had never seen him in his uniform, the scarf tucked inside his shirt that funny way. His hair stood up, stiff as a brush, just as she remembered it, but he had a new look about the eyes.

"You've changed," she said, watching his purposeful movements, as he hung his cap on one of the branching arms above the umbrella-stand, amongst her father's mack and burberry and the old gas-masks.

"So have you," Hank answered. "You've changed back again."

His American intonation sounded beautiful to her. But it was out of place in this house.

"Back again? How do you mean?"

Hank cocked his head, smiling, and looked at her a long time before answering.

"Well, not quite," he said at last. "I mean, you're not really the way you were when you arrived in America. You had pigtails and long brown stockings then."

"But, Hank, that was years ago," Wincy protested. "Little English girls dress that way. I learned a lot about clothes, though, while I was stopping with the Hilliards, mostly from Sally. Don't I—Hank, don't I look different?"

87

Hank laughed. It was nice to hear him laugh again.

"I wasn't thinking of clothes," he said slowly. "It's something in your face that's more—more English. How's everything? What's it like, being back in Oxford?"

Wincy led the way into the drawing-room. Americans were apt to feel chilly in England, even in summer, and a festive moment like this called for a fire, but there was already one in the kitchen.

"Angus and I are jolly glad to be home again," she answered. The polite phrase had become a habit. Then she remembered that she did not have to pretend to Hank. "Well," she added, "Mummie and Daddy are a little hard to please. But they'll get used to us."

The way Hank tucked his legs under the chair when he sat down reminded Wincy of the buffet suppers they used to have in Belmont. He always sat that way, balancing a plate on his knees.

"Oh, Hank, it's wonderful to see you," she told him. "I didn't even know you were in England. Every time I pass an American soldier, I look at him in the hope that he's someone I knew in Belmont. This morning Daddy took us to Magdalen College to hear the May Day singing on the top of the tower. Just as the Latin hymn was floating down, a convoy of American lorries—" she corrected herself hastily, "I mean trucks came over Magdalen Bridge, almost drowning out the music with their noise. Daddy and Angus and I were standing with our bikes under the tower and all of a sudden the truck in front stopped. They all slammed their brakes on. One of the jeeps stopped right next to us. Angus yelled, 'Hiya, sarge,' at the driver and he looked so surprised hearing Angus's American speech. . . ."

Hank laughed. "The singing sounds nifty," he said. "They have a lot of awfully nice customs in England, don't they?"

"Yes. Afterward, we went to see the Morris Dancers. They made Angus and me homesick for our square-dances at home in Belmont. I never dreamed that I'd be seeing you the very same afternoon!"

"I was pretty surprised myself, when my outfit came to England," Hank answered. "Then I got this pass, and there wasn't anything I wanted to see so much as you and Angus."

"Angus will be thrilled, too," Wincy said. "He's gone to the Warden's garden party."

"The Warden? Jail?"

Wincy smiled. "The Warden is the head of Daddy's College," she explained. "A very important person. Mummie was all dressed up and Daddy carried his dogskin gloves. He always takes those yellow gloves to an occasion."

Hank laughed.

"Mummie had managed a frock for me," Wincy added, "what she calls 'something appropriate'—it makes me look thirteen. But I had a headache, so she thought I'd better stop at home."

"Maybe I ought to leave," Hank said, without stirring, "if you're not feeling well."

"Oh, no, I'm quite fit now, really. I have been ever since you came."

And as she spoke, Wincy realized that this was true.

"Were you very anxious to go to the garden party?" Hank asked teasingly. "Psychologists say people sometimes feel sick when they have to do something they don't like."

"You mustn't say 'sick' in England," Wincy corrected,

laughing. "It means lose-your-lunch. Oh, Hank, suppose I'd missed you—you can't imagine how dull it is here."

Hank looked around the room, at the oak settle and the stiff chairs, at the overpowering brown mantelshelf topped by a line of symmetrically hung pictures of the Parthenon.

"I guess it's not so hot," he said with feeling.

"There's no fun, the way there was in Belmont," Wincy said slowly. "Picnics and parties and movies, and music in the house. Maybe if my elder brother were home it would be more that way. But Mummie and Daddy really need us quite badly. Daddy's so helpless. You know—he's a Greek professor."

"I know what you mean," Hank said. "We have some queer dodos at Harvard, too."

"He's not queer, Hank. Don't think that. It's just, being a professor, he doesn't know how to do anything useful, like mending things around the house, or making models with Angus, or playing catch—things like that."

"Uncle Bill's a professor," Hank reminded her.

"Oh, yes, but chemists are different, don't you think, from Greek professors?" Wincy asked earnestly. "Even Mummie isn't very clever at housework. She hardly ever went into the kitchen before the war, so when the maids left, she had a ghastly time. Angus and I do the work since we're home. Even so, Mummie still thinks Angus ought to have a governess."

"Angus? A governess?" Hank snorted. "What does a nine-year-old kid need a nursemaid for? What would Angus do with her? Of course, if she was a good shortstop, and had some commando training—"

"Come in the kitchen and we'll fix some grub," Wincy

said, laughing over her shoulder. She wanted Hank to know she could still speak his language.

The large red tiles in the kitchen floor fascinated Hank.

"This is the first English home I've ever been in," he explained. "I'm seeing you for the first time in your natural habitat. But you were a natural for America, Wincy, once the Hilliards broke you in."

"I loved it," Wincy said, placing a platter of biscuits on the kitchen-table and setting out the tea-things. "You know, I miss the queerest people—people I didn't really care for, like Miss Lowell, my math teacher. And Sandy Whipple—he was that kid the girls used to tease me about. But everybody knew you were the only boy I really liked, Hank, and they couldn't tease me about my foster-cousin. There can't be boy-and-girl stuff between cousins, can there? Not even foster-cousins."

"Can't there be?"

"Of course not," Wincy said flatly, as they sat down, facing each other across the narrow table. She did wish the cups and saucers were nicer. What would Hank think of her home? Coming from America, he wouldn't understand about the war. "Remember that time you took me to a concert at the Fogg?" she asked Hank, giving him his tea.

"You bet—"

"Remember the sodas we had at that little joint in the Square afterwards? You had a black-and-white and I took a strawberry. Gee, we had a good time."

"I remember," Hank answered, looking at her intently in a way Wincy couldn't understand. Then suddenly, he pushed back his chair noisily and stood at attention.

Wincy turned around. Professor and Mrs. Turner were in

the doorway. They looked horrified. Wincy noticed that her father still carried his dogskin gloves.

"Oh, hello," she said weakly. Judging by the look her parents gave her, something must be wrong, but Wincy didn't know what.

"We walked in on tiptoe, Wincy," Mrs. Turner said in an excited tone of voice, "lest you had fallen asleep *nursing that headache*."

The front door slammed. Angus trailed into the passage. Seeing Hank, he took a flying leap between his father and mother and landed with his arms around Hank's neck, his legs curled around Hank's waist, as if he were climbing a tree.

"You old bozo!" he shouted. "Where in the heck did you come from?"

"Don't be rude, Angus," Professor Turner said sharply. He turned to Wincy. "Who is this—gentleman, Wincy?"

"It's Hank, Daddy, Hank Sutton. He lived next door to us in Cambridge. You know—one of the foster-cousins."

"Of course," Mrs. Turner said, with a look of tremendous relief. "It's Mrs. Hilliard's nephew," she reassured her husband.

"That's right," Wincy said, happily.

"The children gave us such disjointed accounts in their little letters," Mrs. Turner told Hank, coming forward and extending her hand, "that we do not have a very clear picture of their life abroad."

"Abroad?" Hank repeated. "Oh—you mean at home."

"In the States," Mrs. Turner explained kindly. "We haven't yet heard all about their friends there. At first we feared you were a total stranger, some soldier Wincy had—well—befriended during our absence, in her queer American way." She looked about the kitchen distastefully. "Shall we go into the drawing room?"

Smiling hopefully, she led the way, but no one followed.

Professor Turner, advancing upon Hank to shake hands belatedly, did not seem to hear.

"Yes," he was saying, "Wincy and Angus had so many friends out there—only this morning Angus mentioned someone I had never heard of before, not one of his New England playfellows, but someone he seemed to cherish nevertheless. Perhaps it was some friend of yours. Charles somebody, an Hibernian name, as I recall it—yes, Charles McCarthy."

"Yes, sir," Hank said, turning to wink at Angus, "he's a friend of mine."

He lifted Angus almost to the ceiling.

"Holy mackerel, kid," he exclaimed, as he set him down again. "You never looked this nifty around Belmont."

Professor Turner seemed astonished. "In what respect, may I ask, was there a difference in the boy's appearance?"

"Well sir," Hank explained, "for one thing, he never wore a necktie."

"Never?"

"And half the time his pants were held up by a bit of string," Hank continued with a grin, "because he couldn't find his belt."

"Had the boy no braces?" the Professor asked. "I hadn't dreamed he had been so neglected."

Wincy's head was beginning to ache again. Hank had only been in England a week. He wasn't on to the ways of English people.

Looking perplexed and grieved, Professor Turner followed his wife into the drawing-room.

Angus was giggling with suppressed wickedness.

"Wait till you hear what Wincy said the other day," he told Hank, as soon as his father was out of the room. "Right in the middle of Mummie's teaparty, she called me a big bum."

Wincy, remembering the painful scene, felt like smacking Angus, but Hank looked at him blankly.

"What of it?" he asked.

"Wincy," Mrs. Turner called from the drawing room, "do bring—bring—Wincy, what *is* his name?"

"Hank, Mummie."

"Not that. I mean his Christian name."

"Harley."

"Do bring Harley in here, dear. It's not the right thing for you to be sitting in the kitchen with him, like a little house-maid entertaining her soldier."

"In Belmont we always sat in the kitchen," Angus began, "when we—"

"Do hush," Wincy snapped, leading the way into the drawing room.

Mrs. Turner waited until everyone was seated and then she took charge of the conversation.

"How old are you, Harley?" she asked. That, Wincy thought, is just what one asks a strange child, when one doesn't know what to say.

"Eighteen, ma'am."

"Indeed! Younger than our boy Mark," Professor Turner remarked. "I fancied you were a good deal older."

"Mark's in the R.A.F. When last we heard, he was in

Africa," Mrs. Turner explained, taking his picture from the writing-desk and showing it to Hank. "What a pity you couldn't have met him, as well as the children."

"Children, Mummie!" Wincy repeated, indignantly. She didn't mind when no one was around, but in front of Hank— Mrs. Turner was unfeeling.

"Yes, my dear," she said, taking the picture from Hank and putting it back on the writing-desk. "For all your pretense to maturity, you are still a child."

"If we had not been obliged to send you out of England because of threatened invasion," the Professor added, "you would still be in the nursery."

"Oh, Daddy, I wouldn't," Wincy insisted.

"Actually, you do seem older than your age," Mrs. Turner admitted. "In the States girls grow up faster. It's such a pity, I always think."

Professor Turner, standing on the cold hearthrug with his hands clasped behind his back, coughed. Wincy knew he was about to make a speech.

"Professor and Mrs. Hilliard had never heard of us," he began, clearing his throat, "when they offered their home to our children. They gave them what appears to have been the most affectionate care. In token of our gratitude, we shall always extend hospitality to any connection of these good people. Harley, we should be delighted if you would stay with us during your leave." He coughed, and smiled warmly at Hank.

"Do," Angus begged, tugging at Hank's sleeve. "You can have Mark's room."

Wincy said nothing. She merely looked at him.

"Thanks," said Hank. "I'd like to stay, but I just got a

twelve-hour pass. We're being shipped out in a couple of days."

"Oh," Wincy said.

Even her mother couldn't think of anything to say then. There was a long, cold quiet. It was Hank who broke the silence with a laugh.

"Imagine being in Africa or one of those hot places on Hallowe'en!" he exclaimed.

Wincy and Angus looked up quickly at the ghastly thought.

"Ah yes," the Professor remarked, "the Eve of All Hallows, the celebration of which—with the cracking of nuts and games utilizing apples—can be traced back to the festival of Pomona and to Druidical ceremonies. In Africa these revelries would hardly be possible."

"In America," Wincy put in eagerly, "they have parties and square-dances."

"We dress up like ghosts," Angus broke in, excitedly. "And rap on windows and ring people's doorbells. If we don't run away, they give us candy."

"Jack-o'-lanterns," Wincy went on, dreamily, "ducking for apples."

"How jolly!" Mrs. Turner said. "You never told us anything about it."

Hank was glancing furtively at his watch.

"Well," he said with a sigh, "guess I've got to be going. Have to get clear back to camp by midnight, and were the connections rotten coming over—" He shook his head gloomily. "Thanks for everything."

When Hank got up, Mrs. Turner led the way into the passage, the others following.

Angus pulled Hank's cap off the rack and held it behind his back.

"Let's have it, kid," Hank said, and Angus reluctantly gave it up. "Good-bye, Mrs. Turner, good-bye, sir."

Wincy pushed past everyone. In a sudden frenzy, she threw her arms around Hank's neck. He held her against his hard chest. The buttons of his blouse dug into her at several points and she felt choked by the acrid smell of his uniform, but she clung to him.

Over his shoulder, Wincy saw her mother's face and knew at once that she had done the wrong thing. When Hank was gone, her mother would very likely be extremely cross, but this time she would not care. It was nothing like that silly business with Francis. Only Hank mattered to her now.

From the doorstep, Wincy watched him hurry along Banbury Road in the hazy twilight. He had crossed to the other side and she could see him over the garden-wall. Half-way down the street, he turned and saluted.

"So long," she called, but her voice did not sound like her own. It was like someone else's, coming from a long way off.

She had a strange feeling, a feeling she had never known before.

XI

WINCY HAD begun playing the fiddle soon after she reached Belmont. When Professor Hilliard had seen how anxious she was to play a real instrument in the orchestra, he had sent her to music-school. It had been fun playing with the Hilliards and Suttons after the buffet supper on Sunday nights. . . .

Family Music, Uncle Bill called it. It was his hobby. He played the first violin, conducting at the same time with wide sweeps of his bow and violent nods of his head. He spent hours copying out music and rearranging it so that the best players would get the hardest parts, but everyone had a bit to play, even Angus and Sutty, even Doctor Sutton, who had never advanced beyond the rattle.

They played everything: Mozart and Haydn Symphonies, Purcell Suites, Overtures to *Pinafore* and *Patience*, along with Uncle Bill's arrangement of Bach Chorales. He had orchestrated their favourite songs, too, like "Carry Me Back to Old Virginny" and "O for the Wings of a Dove."

Perhaps the resulting sounds were not very beautiful, but the players enjoyed themselves, and Uncle Bill never allowed anyone to listen. If there was a visitor, an instrument in keeping with his musical ability was put into his hands, for there were always extra ones about—recorders, the toy trumpet, or merely the triangle or castanets.

"Come on," Uncle Bill would urge, if a visitor were shy, "anyone who can count to four can play in my orchestra."

Sometimes quite good players came in, for the Hilliard Family Music was what you might almost call famous at Harvard. Uncle Bill's young face would light up with happiness then, and he'd bring out the parts for a Brandenburg Concerto or a Holst Suite.

It had been jolly. Wincy had worked hard to learn her parts. Yet she had never practised so eagerly as she did now that she was at home. Not that there was anyone to play with here. Her father and mother did not seem interested in music, although just in the last week or two, they had begun listening to concerts on the wireless.

Since that first afternoon, when she had been interrupted in her playing by the arrival of the Quelches, Wincy had not been asked to perform again. Professor Turner sometimes stuck his head in the crack of the door when she practised. But Wincy's parents were obviously not interested.

So she had taken to practising in the dining room. She could shut the dividing doors, which separated it from the drawing room and be quite alone. After tea, safe within the chocolate-coloured walls, she would take out her violin, and play her way back to the world she loved.

When she played, Wincy could see the Belmont living-room with the frilly white curtains tied back at the windows, and the Suttons and Hilliards sitting around Uncle Bill in an untidy confusion of instrument cases, music stands, and worn manuscript paper, watching for Uncle Bill's downbeat.

Aunt Polly was at the piano, straining forward to see the notes, because she would not wear her new glasses, and Aunt Mary, Hank's mother, stood beside it. She had red hair like Sally's, only darker, and she wore it coiled around her head, like a crown. She played the flute very well and Wincy loved to watch the action of her slender fingers.

Hank played the clarinet. He couldn't always make it be-have—very often such funny squeaks came out of it that the whole orchestra stopped playing to laugh. After running his fingers through his hair impatiently, Hank would blow again.

Their percussion instruments poised in the air, Sutty and Angus and Uncle Harley looked up for the signal to strike, but she, Wincy, was no longer in that section. She sat proudly at the second violin-stand with Sally Sutton.

The day after Hank's visit to Oxford, Wincy went through

her scales and arpeggios with concentration for a little while, but soon found herself wondering whether Hank had been shipped out. Hank fighting, Hank wounded, perhaps, or taken prisoner. . . . She played more slowly, sliding over the notes.

Yesterday at this time, they had been taking tea together in the jolly, warm kitchen. How handsome Hank had looked in his uniform, how nice his American accent sounded! He really hadn't changed so much at all, she thought, tumbling down a scale. Perhaps, if she did well at Newfields, they would let her go to college in America. Radcliffe with Sally Sutton—she'd love it. After that, she could marry Hank and just stay on.

The wings of a dove, she thought, putting her bow down and unconsciously dropping her fingers on the strings in the rhythm of the song. *Far a-way, far a-way would I rove*. But America isn't the wilderness English people think. . . .

Above the daydream, Mrs. Quelch's high-pitched voice, holding forth on the drawing room side of the dividing doors, pushed itself into Wincy's consciousness. She had not heard the lady arrive.

"Not much in the shops for Whitsun," she grumbled.

"I've booked one of Mrs. Trueblood's cockerels," Mrs. Turner said.

"Oh—is she killing them off?" Mrs. Quelch asked, and there was envy in her voice. "You should have notified me when you heard about it, Rachel," she said reproachfully.

Mrs. Turner changed the subject. "What a jolly garden party it was," she exclaimed.

"Nothing like peacetime," Mrs. Quelch complained. "The Warden's getting old. He doesn't look the thing at all. Pinched."

"Yes," Mrs. Turner agreed sadly. "I can't bear to see it. He's quite the nicest man I've ever known, except John. I did want him to see Wincy."

"Pity he didn't," Mrs. Quelch remarked, and Wincy thought there was a disagreeable suggestion in her tone.

But Mrs. Turner was trying to be pleasant. "Brenda looked sweet in her frock," she said. "It will be nice for Wincy having her for a friend and next term they'll be at school together."

Nice, Wincy thought. What a lie—

"I have no doubt," Mrs. Quelch said, "but—I do hope you'll pardon my saying it, Rachel—Winifred seems a bit too forward for Brenda."

"Girls grow up far too fast in the States," Mrs. Turner admitted. "The innocence of youth is tarnished by too much knowledge—of the wrong sort, I mean. There's that thing she calls psychology. I can't help wishing we had kept her at home."

"It all comes of having been frightened by the blitz," Mrs. Quelch exclaimed triumphantly. "Now, I resolved to keep Brenda by my side at all costs. And after all, we weren't invaded. If your Wincy had stopped at home too, she would not now have these wild notions."

Picklepuss, thought Wincy.

"But the stay did do her good in many ways," Mrs. Turner argued, a little timidly. "She learned to be very helpful in the house. She was taught to play the violin amazingly well. In some respects her foster-mother must be a remarkable woman."

"No one," said Mrs. Quelch, "can take a mother's place."

"Or a nannie's," Mrs. Turner added. "That's true."

"Directly a woman gives birth to a child," Mrs. Quelch asserted flatly, "she instinctively becomes knowledgeable concerning it. Now Brenda—"

"I dare say," Mrs. Turner put in, doubtfully, "but I don't feel very knowledgeable about my poppets just at present. Never having had the care of them before, I had no notion what a great many problems they posed. Overwhelming . . ."

"I should speak to Miss Fulleylove," Mrs. Quelch said.

"But it's so near the end of term."

"Nevertheless—," Mrs. Quelch insisted. "Besides, you must be firmer. That's the secret of success in mothercraft. Now, I do think Winifred too much of a child to be entertaining a young man, especially alone in the house. I shouldn't dream of letting Brenda."

"I can't think what you mean," Mrs. Turner said sharply, then added laughing, "Oh, *that*—it's so long ago, I had forgotten the little incident. But I put a stop to it directly. You see, as it happens, I actually was at home at the time, up in the nursery. I shouldn't say Wincy was entirely to blame. Your Francis invited her."

If anyone was to blame, Wincy thought, it was Mummie.

"Francis?" Mrs. Quelch repeated, her voice rising. "Indeed, it wasn't Francis we saw embracing Winifred in the doorway yesterday on our way to the garden party. It was a tall, dark boy, my dear Rachel, in uniform. An American, I suspect . . ."

There was a hush. Mrs. Turner did not seem to be able to answer back.

Why didn't she tell her that he was only a foster-cousin? Wincy wondered. Didn't she know there isn't any boy-girl stuff between cousins? That would fix Picklepuss, the old cat. Why didn't Mummie stand up for her?

"That was Harley Sutton," Mrs. Turner said shakily, "Mrs. Hilliard's nephew. He landed in England with his outfit last week and came to see the children on his sight-seeing leave."

"Indeed?" Mrs. Quelch remarked, full of interest. "But such a warm embrace . . . I'm surprised you didn't stop at home to greet him, Rachel. All the way from the States—"

"We had no idea he was coming," Mrs. Turner explained hastily. "The boy never thought to telephone. Wincy just happened to be at home, as she had a headache, and I considered it unwise to take her into the crush at the Warden's."

"Quite. But what a coincidence—" she drew out the words sententiously, "her headache, and this young soldier's visit."

"I can't think what you mean," Mrs. Turner cried angrily.

"Can't you? Mrs. Quelch's rasping voice was like honey now. "Our generation had headaches too, Rachel, when we were young, and eager for forbidden fruit. Had you forgotten, my dear? I should have thought you more astute."

Wincy was furious. The snake, she gasped, the snake . . .

She looked about the room for something to throw, a good, solid object.

No, she thought, that won't do. But I'll open the dividing door and tell the reptile to her face what I think of her, even if Mummie brains me.

The serpent, she said, her hand cold on the china knob.

And then, as a brilliant surprise, it came to her—how you handled a snake. You didn't talk to it—that showed no understanding of psychology at all—you charmed it, cast a spell with music.

With dramatic suddenness, Wincy threw open the door.

Mrs. Quelch, sitting on the window-seat, erect and self-possessed, did not have a chance to say a word, for Wincy fixed her eye upon her and instantly began playing.

O for the wings, for the wings of a dove, she played with long, sweeping bows and a sustaining vibrato.

Far a-way, far a-way would I rove, she went on, pouring hot fury into the music. *In the wilderness build me a nest* . . .

Like a boa-constrictor who has raised himself to strike and then thought better of it, Mrs. Quelch shrank back amongst the cushions. Under Wincy's spell-binding stare, she dropped her eyes. She looked quite frightened. When Wincy and Mendelssohn and the Psalmist had done with her, Mrs. Quelch was nothing but a crumpled old gossip with her hat knocked crooked.

Intent on Mrs. Quelch, Wincy did not see her mother's face. She drew her bow slowly through the last beat, then, as suddenly as she had opened it, she shut the door.

After that, the tears spilled over.

But Mrs. Quelch never knew about them. Bringing her visit to a close without another word, she removed herself into the passage, probably inching like a snake, Wincy thought. Had she put her hat to rights?

By the time Mrs. Quelch reached the door, she had got herself in hand sufficiently to fling one more dart at Mrs. Turner. "Quite a talented girl, my dear, really," she said. "That would, of course, account for her irregular conduct. We all know artists are given to that sort of thing, don't we? *Good* day, Rachel."

Through the bow-window, Wincy watched Mrs. Quelch inching down Banbury Road.

XII

"YOUR MOTHER tells me—" Professor Turner began, as he was leaving the house two days later, and stopped. He wiped the beads of perspiration off his nose.

Something's coming, Wincy thought. Something bad—

"Your mother tells me," Professor Turner began again, "that Miss Fulleylove finds your history preparation at Agassiz deplorably inadequate. She says you will have a deal of work catching up your form."

"I know," Wincy said, relieved to find it was nothing more than history which had upset her father, "but there's the whole summer. I can make it up."

"Actually," Professor Turner began, and looked helplessly toward the door, as if hoping his wife would come home in time to assist him, "we—your mother and I—consider it advisable that you enter school at once."

"But, Daddy, it's almost June. School only lasts a few weeks more. It isn't worth it and I'd hate to go before I'd made up the history."

"Quite. I will not conceal the fact that I am in full agreement with you on that point, but the matter has been decided, so let us not discuss it further. I regret that you apportioned so much of your time to the study of chemistry at Agassiz, instead of to history, which would be of benefit to you now. But I suppose you were unduly influenced by Professor Hilliard."

"It was my elective course," Wincy argued.

"Elective," the Professor repeated impatiently. "Too much was left to your own judgment and fancies. A child needs guidance. Even my undergraduates would be incapable of choosing their studies wisely."

"Maybe," Wincy admitted. "I don't know them. But in America they'd have to make up their own schedule."

"*Schedule*," her father corrected, pronouncing it the English way, "but what you really mean is timetable."

"Okay," Wincy answered indifferently.

"Throughout these last dreadful years," Professor Turner was saying earnestly, "when we were concerned for Mark's safety, for the whole structure of British life, I have withdrawn more and more from a world that is obviously being destroyed by science into the serene domain of antiquity."

He looked sad, almost old, as he left for Home Guard. Wincy wondered how things were going at St. James's. If only she could find out what was wrong—

The serene domain of antiquity, she repeated to herself, flopping down on the monk's bench. Men fought in those days, too, without scientific weapons—I know that much, even if Miss Fulleylove thinks I'm behind in history. They just ran people through with javelins, or poured nice molten lead down on them from towers.

Now she was supposed to go to school. Whatever for, in May? Nothing made sense. But she wasn't going to go to school, because she really could make the history up faster by herself, during the long vac. Dear old Daddy, in his serene domain of antiquity, didn't know half what was happening around him.

If only there were someone young in the house to talk to, someone who would see things as she did, like Sally or Hank Sutton. Mark, perhaps . . .

She had never known her elder brother very well. He was

quiet, and always so busy with tennis or punting when he was home from Winchester that he never seemed to have time for ragging in the nursery. When she and Angus left for America, he was fifteen and all wrapped up in his own affairs. In a way, he was a stranger, much more distant than the Suttons now, but if only he were home, Wincy was sure they would be good friends. They would share the things which old people, like parents, couldn't understand.

But surely, about school, Mummie would understand. Wincy remembered how tenderly distressed she had looked that night when the Warden sent for Professor Turner—the night she and Angus came home from America. "I do so wish I could help you," she had said. She would certainly help Wincy because, not being a don, she would understand that there was no point at all in going to school just for a month or so.

What is it they call that term again—the fall, no, autumn term? she asked herself. Michaelmas, that's it. I'll start in Michaelmas term with my history all made up. Maybe I'll choose Ancient, just to please Daddy—that is, if they let me fix my own *schedule*, even if the "girls your age" Mummie is always talking about don't do that in England.

"I'm not 'girls-your-age,' " Wincy said quite emphatically to the monk's bench. "I'm me—I mean I."

She hated to think of all those "girls your age" whose eyes would pop when she entered the schoolroom. Wincy remembered her very first day at Newfields. Nannie, pushing Angus in the pram, had taken her as far as the door. The courtyard of the school was cluttered with blue and brown nannies. Up to the last minute, she had clung to Nannie's warm, brown safeness. Then she had been firmly pushed into school.

In Belmont, the first day had been less frightening. By that time she was not quite so scared. She had simply gone along with Sally Sutton. Everyone was extremely kind, but it was a long time before they called her anything but the Little English Girl.

What would they call her at Newfields? An evacuee? Well, she wasn't going to school, anyhow, till Michaelmas term. That was absolutely flat.

And, having made the decision, Wincy felt better. She hopped off the monk's bench to begin the history at once. Running upstairs, two steps at a time, she had almost reached the landing when the front door opened. Wincy turned round and saw Mrs. Turner come in carrying a large bundle of clothing.

"Hello, Mummie," Wincy called and darted down again.

Her mother looked nice, with her fresh, pink cheeks and golden hair. She was a lot prettier than Aunt Polly, even in her W.V.S. hat.

"I got them," she announced, her eyes shining, and dropped the bundle on the monk's bench, "at the Clothing Exchange—just what you need. Not new, of course, but in very good condition."

Wincy was dying to know what "they" were, but her mother hurried on.

"I know it will be disagreeable getting used to other people's things, dear, but we all must now, and, as they say at the W.V.S., 'there's enough to go round if only it's exchanged often enough.'" She looked pityingly at Wincy. "You've been accustomed to such heaps of new frocks, I know it will be hard. I *am* sorry."

"I don't mind a bit," Wincy said. "All Sally's clothes were so nice, I couldn't wait to get them."

"It would have been wicked to spend coupons on a school-uniform," Mrs. Turner went on, opening the bundle and displaying a mass of navy blue serge, "and that travelling-costume you wore home would have been quite out of place in Oxford, so I put it down in the Barter Book and got these instead—just what you need."

"You mean you gave my suit away?" Wincy cried. "The suit Aunt Polly bought me?"

"Yes, dear. You don't mind, do you?" Mrs. Turner looked at Wincy in surprise. "Oh, darling, you do—" she exclaimed. "I never thought of asking you. Nannie always took care of your clothes without consulting you. It seemed quite natural for me—I thought I was being frightfully clever, getting these things." She looked hurt. "Darling, I'm ever so sorry," she went on, looking at Wincy tenderly. "You know, sometimes I forget that you're not a little poppet any more."

"It's okay," Wincy muttered.

But it wasn't. Maybe the suit was out of place in Oxford. Aunt Polly really had wanted her to choose a beige one, and she should have done it. Only, this shade of purple was popular at Agassiz. She wouldn't have worn the suit here, but she didn't want to give it away, either. She would have been perfectly happy, just having it hang in her wardrobe . . .

Instead, she now had a school-uniform, which she couldn't use.

"It's okay," she repeated, eyeing the blue serge with disgust. "But I don't need a uniform yet. I'm going to make up the history by myself."

"I shouldn't worry about it too much, chicken," Mrs. Turner said comfortingly. "Miss Fulleylove says the form-mistress, whatever her name is, will help you. Miss Pusey—that's it. She knows you're at a disadvantage, having been in America."

It was as simple as that. If you were on the fence about a thing, it was easy for older people to push you over, but once you had made a decision and showed you meant it, they were usually ready to co-operate. It didn't matter about the suit, just so she didn't have to go to school—she couldn't have worn it, anyway. Besides, she had plenty of other nice clothes—Sally's dirndl and lots of others.

Now she must show she meant well and get to work at once. Wincy put her arm around her mother's waist, trying to squeeze onto the same stair with her as they went up together.

"I'm so glad you understand," she said happily. "I'll start working right away."

"You're being sensible about the costume," Mrs. Turner said, giving Wincy a little pat. "With clothing so short, we cannot be too concerned about personal wishes. Wait dear," she asked, following Wincy into her room, "I must see how the gym tunic fits."

"There's no point in it—if it's right now, it won't fit when I start school in September, at the rate I'm growing."

"I hope it's right now," Mrs. Turner answered, "because you're starting school tomorrow. I told Miss Fulleylove this morning."

"I don't want to," Wincy explained. "There's no use going to school just for a few weeks."

"Yes there is," Mrs. Turner insisted. "You will be looked after there. If we had Nannie, or even maids, I shouldn't urge you. But I cannot keep my eye on you. Just at present I'm frightfully occupied, collecting books for the military camps, and my knitting party is swamped with work."

Wincy looked at her mother earnestly. "You needn't keep your eye on me," she said. "I'll study by myself, I really will."

"I'm not afraid you'll scamp," Mrs. Turner said. "It's in other ways that you need watching."

"We often stayed alone at the Hilliards," Wincy argued.

"I dare say," Mrs. Turner answered, and Wincy thought she sounded a little bitter. "Your behaviour indicates neglect. But at Newfields you will be kept from running off the lines. When you come home, there will be prep and then it will be bedtime."

Wincy could see the days stretched in an endless chain before her—school, prep and bedtime, school, prep and bedtime. . . . What a prospect!

"Now, try these on," Mrs. Turner was saying, as she dumped the serge mass onto Wincy's bed.

And before she knew it, her mother slid down the zipper of Sally Sutton's skirt, and was gently pulling her sweater off over her head, as if she were still a little girl.

"These shirts are good pre-war pongee," Mrs. Turner was saying happily. "One can't get material like it nowadays." She fastened the tunic under Wincy's arm and knotted a cord around her waist, like a nun's.

"You will be in Brenda Quelch's form," Mrs. Turner said

soothingly, as she tied the blue-and-gold Newfields scarf under Wincy's chin. She looked at Wincy's face, expecting it to be radiant at the news, and added in the same cheery voice, "It will be so nice for you to be chums with her again, the way you were before you were evacuated."

Wincy stretched her neck. The knot was not really tight, but it felt disagreeable, and she gulped, mostly to keep down her anger. She had always hated mannish clothes. A good thing Hank hadn't caught her in this revolting outfit. . . .

"You look very nice now," Mrs. Turner said, inspecting Wincy. "If your hair were shorter, you'd look quite English. But," she added with a warm smile, "those American shoes will be the envy of Newfields School."

Wincy said nothing. She was miserable, that was all. Miserable—

"No doubt the blazer will fit, too," Mrs. Turner said confidently, nodding toward the jacket on the bed as she left the room.

Who cares whether it does? Wincy thought angrily.

So that was it—she was being sent to school for safe-keeping, to jail—she who had journeyed all the way to America and back with a small boy to look after. Miss Fulleylove would see that she didn't go on the River . . .

Not that she cared about Francis, anyhow. She hoped never to see him again after the way her mother had embarrassed her, calling to him out of the window and sending him off, like a little kid. What would he think of her now, in these weeds, with all her glamour gone? He probably couldn't tell her apart from Brenda. Hank and Sally would just hoot if they saw her looking this way.

She wondered what Mark would think, if he should suddenly come popping in the front door. Would he like her, regardless—just because she was his sister? He had never been friendly when they were younger, but it would be different now, more like Hank and Sally. She did need a friend to talk things over with. There was no chance, though, of Mark's popping in.

No one said very much about the war, yet there was a new feeling of chill in the house, like you felt when you walked into one of those American air-conditioned trains— unnatural cold clinging to everything—now that there was less fog over the Channel. There was talk of large-scale bombing and some people thought invasion of the Continent might start this summer. No one really knew, but the Turners were sure of one thing: whatever did take place, Mark would be in the thick of it.

In the little mirror on the highboy in front of the window, Wincy found to her surprise that she looked quite nice. But the mirror only reflected her head, which hadn't changed. Wincy felt better. With the bob and the perm she had got before leaving Belmont, the uniform might not matter very much, after all.

But when she went into her father's dressing-room and looked at herself in the long cheval-glass, she was crushed. One look and she knew the uniform was worse, far worse than she had feared.

Except for her height, and the bulges which had appeared in America, she was the same pathetic sight she had been when she was evacuated—worse. She looked ridiculously overgrown. The gym tunic, reaching no further than the top of her knees, hung straight from her shoulders, tied in the middle like a sack of grain. In her cleverly tailored American clothes, the bulges were pretty well concealed, but in this thing they stuck out like the humps of a camel.

It was more than she could bear. She crumpled on the floor at the foot of the mirror, pulling the skirt as far over her knees as it would go. She wished the ship had been torpedoed on the journey home. Only then, Angus would have drowned, too . . .

In one corner of the mirror, her father had stuck a snap-shot one of the kids had taken of her under the big maple at Agassiz. Wincy was wearing that lovely flowered playsuit Aunt Polly had bought her at Filene's.

Aunt Polly wouldn't have stuffed her into an awful-look-ing thing like this gym tunic, just because other girls wore them. Aunt Polly always said it didn't matter how you looked to other people, so long as you yourself were pleased with your appearance. Now there was nothing left to her looks, except her hair.

But as she turned her head from side to side in the glass to console herself, she discovered that even her wave wasn't nice any more. The ends of the curls were beginning to strag-gle.

Nothing was nice any more.

June

XIII

THE TELEGRAM came on the Saturday while the Turners were at breakfast. Wincy brought it into the dining room.

Mrs. Turner glanced at the message quickly and gave a little cry. "Mark—" she gasped pitifully. Handing the telegram to her husband without meeting his eyes, she went to the window and stood looking out, her head turned away.

"Missing," the Professor explained briefly, looking over the paper at Wincy.

He got up and went to his wife. In the instant when he looked at the telegram, his face seemed to change completely. It was as if the flesh had evaporated, leaving the skin drawn white over the skull and sharpening his nose.

There they stood—no words, no tears—looking out into the garden.

Wincy felt horror creep through her as she saw her father's face shrink. Angus was clutching her arm, looking terrified. But he had the sense to keep still. Good kid—

Wincy glanced through the dividing doors at Mark's photograph on the writing-desk. She tried to picture him as he had looked when she and Angus left Oxford for Liverpool. He had been fifteen then, and did not seem at all interested in his sister and brother. But he must have cared more than she realized, for he had been at the station to see them off, looking quite tall beside their father. Wincy remembered the slope of his shoulders in his cricket-blazer, his fair hair and calm Turner eyes.

Yet, even as she had been unable to picture her parents before she saw them again, Wincy could only remember the shape of Mark's features in a far away sort of dimness. There was no motion, no life in the shapes.

Strange that Francis, whom she did not care about at all, should be so vivid in her mind, while her own brother was so vague. . . . Even Hank, whom Wincy had seen only a month ago, and whom she cared for so very, very much, was beginning to fade a little. It would have helped to have his picture. Was *he* safe?

Maybe that was the way that people looked when they were dead—simply a far away sort of dimness, without motion, without life.

Wincy pulled Angus gently into the passage. "Don't speak to them," she whispered. "Just keep still."

"What is it?" he asked, still clinging to her.

"Something's happened to Mark—something terrible. Just don't bother them." She bent down and rubbed her cheek against Angus's soft hair. It had been cut by a British barber after it had grown in.

Professor and Mrs. Turner made no sound. They must still be standing there by the window. Wincy and Angus sat down on the monk's bench to wait. They did not know what to do.

Tigger, the dog across the way, had been run down by a motor-car when Wincy was about ten. They had seen it lying in the road when they walked home from school. Nannie, who was not so quick, hadn't noticed anything unusual until they were almost upon the little body, lying with its head

thrown back and paws outstretched. Then, in great con-
sternation, she bustled her charges into the house, shocked
that she had allowed them to look upon death.

Angus crowded against Wincy. His forehead was puckered and there was a desperate expression on his face, as
though he were trying to figure out a way to fix things.

The blood was beating in Wincy's head and she was afraid
she was going to be sick.

It seemed a long time before there was any sound in the
dining room. Then Mrs. Turner came into the passage. "Oh,"
she exclaimed suddenly, seeing Wincy and Angus there, "you
poor little souls, I'd forgotten about you. My poor babies—"
And to Wincy's astonishment, she burst into tears, running
upstairs as fast as she could.

In the dining room she had been so brave, standing by the
window and looking out into the garden. She hadn't even
sobbed. Why, Wincy wondered, should her mother cry because she and Angus were sitting quietly in the passage.

It almost seemed as though she, Wincy, were the mother,
and her mother were a little girl in need of comfort. And
Daddy, with his shrunken face—but what could one do?
What?

"Come on," Wincy said to Angus. "I'll take Mummie's job
and you do Daddy's. I think he's the washer-up this week."

They kept the house going all day, she and Angus. They
even did the "weekly shop," standing in line for hours without knowing what there was at the end. But Mrs. Turner was
satisfied when they returned and showed her how much food
they had managed to get.

As Mrs. Palmer across the street had offered to take Mrs.
Turner's place at the W.V.S. that afternoon, Professor

Turner persuaded his wife to rest in a deck-chair after tea while he thinned the carrots and tied up the scarlet runners. He looked more himself again.

"Your Roi-de-Dijon roses are doing well this year," he called to Mrs. Turner across the garden, and she nodded, trying to look pleased.

Wincy watched from the French windows in the drawing room. The trowel looked odd in Professor Turner's hand. Books were the only objects Wincy associated with him. Nevertheless, he was a good gardener. He had produced an abundance in his tiny vegetable plot.

Now that Mrs. Turner was relaxing, the strain had gone out of her face a bit. She looked very sad, but she could smile when her husband turned to her, as he did every few moments, to telegraph reassurance.

They were nice together, Wincy thought. They could fall back on each other in time of trouble and they both had guts. It must have been this way when they sent her and Angus to an unknown home across the ocean, but then Wincy hadn't understood. She had only seen their brave smiles and never suspected how they must be crying inside. "People of good taste don't display emotion," Mrs. Turner had once said when Wincy asked her to show Angus more affection.

Now, as Wincy watched her father send those loving messages with his eyes, she knew her parents felt much more than they ever showed.

"John," Mrs. Turner said suddenly, sitting up, "I fear we've let Wincy and Angus become aware of our anxiety over Mark. Children shouldn't be allowed to feel these things."

"They're not such children," the Professor answered, as he scraped the earth from his trowel. "Wincy's a woman, actually. I don't think you appreciate how responsible she is. And Angus is capable of sharing the family burden, too. It's not the way it was when we were children, Rachel. I shouldn't fear," he added soothingly.

"They looked so forlorn when I found them on the monk's bench," Mrs. Turner said. "Poor babies—but you're right about their growing up. It's those lost years that the little ones were away that confuse me, I suppose. And Mark's been gone two now. Oh, John, it doesn't seem as though our children could be—" Her words were carried away by the breeze.

Wincy, standing by the French windows in the drawing room, felt pleased. Daddy really did understand about her age and he was bringing Mummie around, too. In many ways, Wincy felt older than her parents.

Strange voices came from the passage. There were visitors. Angus had opened the door to them. The Warden of St. James's had come with his daughter, as well as Doctor Quelch and some of the Fellows.

When Professor Turner came in from the garden to greet the visitors, Wincy noticed that he unconsciously wiped his hands on his trousers, as Angus did at table. She could see, too, that he was very much touched by the Warden's visit.

" 'Non, si male nunc, et olim sic erit,' " the old gentleman said, clasping Professor Turner's hand warmly.

As Angus was standing by, the Professor seemed to feel it his duty to give his son an English version of the Warden's sympathetic words.

" 'If we fare ill today,' " he translated, " ' 'twill not always be so,'—Horace."

The Warden smiled down on Angus from a great height and patted his shoulder. He wore a parson's collar, and he was so old that he had an almost childlike face.

So that's the Warden, Wincy said to herself—not at all frightening. The way Daddy talked, I thought he must be terrifying. Rather sweet, as a matter of fact, more like a baby, so pink and gentle, and those pale blue eyes—

The visitors walked through the window to the garden. More people arrived—Mrs. Palmer, who reported about the work at the W.V.S., and Mrs. Quelch with Francis.

Evidently, they had all come because of the dreadful news about Mark, but the odd thing was, they never mentioned him at all. Queer, Wincy thought—they must all be people of very good taste . . .

Probably fearing more Latin, Angus retreated to the bottom of the garden. Wincy stood by the herb-bed alone, feeling quite out of things. All these strange people . . . The Warden's daughter looked very nice. She wore her hair wound in a crown around her head and she had lovely grey eyes, but she must be at least twenty, so she was not likely, Wincy thought, to notice her.

If only Aunt Polly could suddenly turn up, or Sally Sutton, or Hank! Hank might really come—he had once. She felt so lonely and depressed that she wanted to run indoors, but she knew that that would be considered rude. Her head was still pounding. "I wish someone would come and talk to me," she said to herself.

Francis suddenly stood before her, his face white and earnest.

"Did you read the telegram?" he asked softly. "What did it say?"

Francis and Mark had been chums, though Francis was younger. Wincy wondered whether that was why he was being nice to her now.

"Missing," she answered. Her father and mother had not explained the details to her. Suddenly her heart jumped. "Could that mean that Mark isn't—dead?"

"It could," Francis said. "No one knows yet—"

"Oh, Francis!" she exclaimed in unspeakable relief.

"We'll have to wait," he said. His expression changed. "It makes me boil," he added, looking very fierce. "Why won't Father let me join up?"

It was as good as having someone from Belmont to talk to, Wincy thought. Since Francis had spoken to her, the beating in her head had eased.

"Oh, Francis—" Wincy exclaimed again, and in her pleasure at having him talk so candidly to her and her relief at what he had said about Mark, she clutched his hand.

Mrs. Quelch was watching. She stood beside the rosebushes talking to the Warden, but she looked directly at Wincy.

Wincy dropped Francis's hand quickly. He must have noticed his mother, too, for he hurried off to speak to Professor Turner.

Wincy was alone again.

Someone said, "Your father tells me you are a budding musician, Winifred."

Turning, Wincy found that the Warden had moved over to talk to her. "Do you play?" she asked shyly.

"Not the fiddle. Before the war, we used to have a great deal of music in our college," he said, looking back through time with those pale blue eyes. "I hope it can be revived."

"Why not?" Wincy asked.

"It all depends," the Warden said, almost to himself. "If one of those dashed unmusical Fellows succeeds me—"

Wincy did not know whether Doctor Quelch was musical. She watched him standing at the bottom of the garden talking to Mrs. Turner, his important nose silhouetted against the brick wall. He certainly didn't look musical, but you couldn't go by looks.

"What instrument do you play?" Wincy asked the Warden.

"Flute, my dear, that mellifluous instrument . . ." he answered, smiling.

Wincy thought of Aunt Mary, Hank's mother—how she used to play the leading part in the Mozart Flute Quartets and the cuckoo in Haydn's *Toy Symphony*.

"Oh," Wincy exclaimed happily, before she stopped to think whom she was addressing, "you could be the cuckoo."

"The what?" the old gentleman demanded, pretending to look offended.

"The cuckoo," Wincy repeated. "Don't you know the *Toy Symphony*?"

The old gentleman's eyes took on that distant expression again, as though he were looking back through time. "Do you mean that symphony Haydn wrote for a lark?" he asked. "Where part of the orchestra uses toy instruments—the nightingale and quail and so on?"

"Yes," Wincy said happily. She had begun to fear no one in Oxford knew the music she had played at the Hilliards'.

"Once, long ago, we performed it at a gaudy," the Warden said. "At that time we had a number of musical Fellows in the College. They wore eighteenth-century costumes with wigs and tried to reproduce faithfully the spirit of the work. It was a huge success. The audience laughed till it wept, and so did the players."

"We have the nightingale here," Wincy said eagerly. "It was Angus's part when we played the symphony in Belmont —our home in America, you know. He loved the nightingale so much that our foster-father let him take it when we came back to Oxford. He dribbles frightfully down his front, but he comes in on the right beat every time."

The Warden laughed. "It's a jolly work," he recalled.

Wincy forgot what an important personage the Warden was. He was so nice and seemed so interested that she went on to tell him about the other music they used to play in Uncle Bill's orchestra, how even Sutty and Angus were allowed to join in, even Uncle Harley, who couldn't play anything more than the rattle.

"What a happy experience you had abroad—" the Warden said, listening eagerly. "Have you met Daphne? She plays the 'cello. You might do something together." He went off to detach his daughter from Mrs. Quelch's conversation.

Wincy had been watching Daphne out of the side of her eye all afternoon. She had been hoping someone would introduce her and now, when the Warden brought her over, she was so happy that she feared her eagerness showed too much.

"This is my daughter Daphne," the Warden said, presenting her to Wincy as if Wincy were equally grown up. "Do get Winifred to tell you about her jolly times in America, Daphne," he urged, walking off to speak to Mrs. Turner.

"Are you a musician?" Wincy asked shyly. She liked this girl. She wanted to be liked by her.

"Oh, no," Daphne answered, "but I used to play quite a lot, when I was at Somerville. We had wonderful times. Now I keep house for Father and help the Head Almoner at the Radcliffe."

"Radcliffe?" Wincy repeated, dazed.

She knew Daphne was not referring to Sally Sutton's college in Cambridge, U.S.A., but that was what she saw in her mind when Daphne spoke—the peaceful yard as it looked from the Brattle Street gate where she and Sally used to gaze hopefully as they went by. Sally was actually there now, and Wincy meant to join her as soon as the war was over. She had not told her parents about it yet, but she was going.

Daphne described her duties at the Radcliffe Infirmary, but Wincy was still standing on Brattle Street in Cambridge, just below the Longfellow House, looking across at the stone marker which indicated the spot where, under the spreading chestnut tree, the village smithy stood. . . .

Warden Godstow had come to take his daughter home.

"Come to tea on Sunday," Daphne said cordially. "We'll play duets or sing madrigals: *Sing We and Chant It* and *Strike It Up, Tabor.*"

Wincy had never heard of these songs.

"It was a joy hearing about the music in the States," the Warden said in parting.

"I wish Mummie and Daddy cared for that sort of thing," Wincy said sadly. "It would help now."

"Pity they aren't musical," the Warden agreed, adding, "We must think of some means of distracting them until better news arrives."

"Then you think, too, that maybe Mark isn't dead?" Wincy asked suddenly. "Oh, Warden—"

Finally, the visitors left. The Quelches were the last to go. Professor Turner had ushered them out and was just going to collapse on the chair in the bow-window when he noticed something outside that made him jump up again.

"By jove!" he exclaimed, and Wincy, rushing to the window to find out what had caused the ejaculation, saw a procession of old ladies coming down Banbury Road carrying stirrup-pumps. "I'd forgotten the old ladies," the Professor explained. "This was the day I had promised to practise their pumps with them."

The ladies had reached the garden-gate. Wincy noticed that her father looked exhausted, but he straightened his jacket and went out to do his job. There was no time in England for a man to sit alone with his grief. His son's plane might have exploded in midair, or fallen into the sea, or—at best—been brought down in enemy territory. He might be wounded, imprisoned, dead. . . . But the fire-fighters must go on with their training.

"What I want to know, Professor," Wincy heard the most ancient of the ladies asking, as they passed under the bow-window on their way through the garden, "is how long an incendiary goes on burning."

"I don't know, I'm sure," the Professor answered wearily.

"But if you can't tell me how long a bomb burns, Professor," the ancient lady said querulously, "how am I to know when it's out?"

Wincy saw her father, intent on examining the nozzle of a pump, suddenly throw back his head and laugh.

Somehow, the foolish woman had helped.

XIV

St. James's College, while one of the smaller foundations in the University, is very rich in tradition. The Hall, built on the site of the original one which was destroyed during the reign of Bloody Mary, is not even four centuries old, but the Chapel dates from an early period.

Or perhaps it's the other way round, Wincy thought. I never really listened when Daddy used to tell visitors—

All through its long history, the College took pride in being the last to introduce reforms. Resisting innovation— "Never yield" is St. James's motto—the members of the College seemed always to be one generation behind the times, a fact which gave them a decided advantage over their contemporaries in mastering history and the classics.

It wouldn't do in science, Wincy thought.

She entered the great oaken portal of St. James's the day after the bad news about Mark had arrived and crossed the College Gardens on her way to tea with Daphne Godstow.

A crowd of little boys in grey flannels came rushing through the cloisters on their way to choir-practice. They scurried along without the rough-housing Wincy expected to see, but she thought they had quite jolly faces, even if they were going to church.

Wincy had not been in the Chapel since she was small. Her mother insisted on taking her and Angus to the morning service at St. Giles, but she did not ask them to accompany her to Evening Prayers at the College.

Church bored Wincy. The music was nice, but she was always aware of a depressing constraint left over from childhood, as though Nannie were still sitting in the pew beside her, nudging her to begin the hymn, or else to get up or sit down, regulating Wincy's movements with jerks of her heavy eyebrows.

Wincy had explained all this to Aunt Polly when she first got to Belmont, and Aunt Polly had seemed to understand at once. She had said that she thought religion was not necessarily a matter of going to church, but of one's feeling for one's fellow men, that goodness was not a state of being, but of doing.

Warden House appeared beyond the rosebushes at the bottom of the Gardens. Behind it, Wincy could see the meadows stretching all the way down to the Cherwell. The walls of the house were covered with creeper, making it look stately, and yet it was homey, too, with the border of blue lupin and columbine under the little leaded windows and the Warden's bicycle parked beside the drive.

Wincy laughed when she passed the bicycle. Since the blackout, the Warden had painted "The Lord is my Light" on the place where the lamp should have been.

Daphne came to the door and welcomed Wincy. She seemed so pleased to see her that Wincy felt a sudden glow of happiness.

"Any news?" Daphne asked anxiously, as they sat down on the window-seat in the low, panelled library.

"No," Wincy answered. "Do you think it will come now before the end of the war? It's so dreadful for Mummie and Daddy, not knowing."

Daphne put her hand on Wincy's for a moment and looked at her fondly. Then she talked of other things. She wanted to know all about Wincy's life abroad.

Wincy found herself telling her new friend about the Hilliards and the Suttons and how nice it was in Belmont. She even told about Hank's visit the day of the garden party.

While Daphne made tea, Wincy looked through the casement windows across the garden and the meadows to a bend of the Cherwell. Someone had taken her paddling in a canoe there once when she was very small.

"It's lovely here, too," she said suddenly, as Daphne came in with a tray.

"Been a wee bit homesick, haven't you?" Daphne asked. Then, seeing a guilty look on Wincy's face, she added quickly, "I know precisely how it feels. I still miss my friends at Somerville, though it's been two years since we took our degrees and went to our different war jobs. I'm the only one left in Oxford."

"Did you all study Greek and Latin and those dry subjects?"

"Not all. One of my friends was interested in chemistry, another in psychology. I studied musicology."

"Oh," Wincy exclaimed, amazed. "I didn't think people did in England. Especially psychology. The English don't seem to know much about it."

Daphne looked surprised. "Have you talked to Doctor Wilson? He's doing some very interesting experiments at the laboratory," she said.

"No," Wincy answered. "I was afraid nobody here understood about complexes. The way my parents handle Angus, he'll be ridden with them in a year. Of course, my parents aren't used to children—they're only beginners—"

Daphne laughed. "I believe you'll educate them," she said gaily. Then she became earnest. "By complexes, do you mean something like an undue attachment for one's parents, or a sense of inadequacy?"

"Yes." Wincy was pleased. Daphne actually did know a lot about these things, though she hadn't got the names right. Perhaps after all, most English people had the same ideas as Americans. Perhaps it was only her parents who were behind the times.

Daphne sat thinking, looking out across the College Gardens. She was very pretty, Wincy thought, with her calm, intelligent, grey eyes and her hair wound in a crown about her head.

"Well, no," Daphne said at length. "English people don't bother their heads about that sort of thing as a rule, though before the war, when there wasn't so much to do, some scientists did. But we don't have to worry much about complexes. We dispose of that sort of thing at birth."

Wincy looked up in astonishment. "At birth?" she asked, incredulously. "But how can one? I mean, one hasn't even got the complexes yet."

"Baptism," Daphne explained in her gentle voice, but not as though she were talking to a child. "Baptism rids people of original sin and leaves them free to go about the business of life. It's much more expedient than psycho-analysis. I understand it takes years to rid a person of complexes, and even then they may return."

It was a new idea, and quite good, Wincy considered. She wasn't sure. If only she could have learned more about psychology before she left America—she realized now that she didn't know enough to help in even a simple argument like this.

Daphne stood up and collected the tea-things. "You're an

interesting person," she said frankly. "It's fun to come up against new ideas, and one isn't so apt to get them stopping at home. You've been very fortunate, haven't you?"

Wincy looked up with a grateful expression. No one else in England had seemed to think that she'd been fortunate in going to America.

"Brenda Quelch feels no end sorry she didn't go when all those children were sent overseas," Daphne said. "Since you came home, she wishes she'd been, too, though she didn't want to go at the time."

"Oh," Wincy said in surprise. It had never occurred to her that Brenda might feel anything but superior to her.

It was time for Evening Prayers. Wincy could see the undergraduates coming from their rooms and strolling across the lawns in the late sunlight.

"By Jove, it's time already," Daphne said, hurrying out with the tray. "I'd no idea it was so late—I was so engrossed in all your ideas. We didn't even sing madrigals, so you must come again next Sunday."

Wincy stood uncertainly by the door. Did Daphne mean that she wished her to go home now? She hated leaving. It had been the happiest afternoon she had spent since she left Belmont. And next Sunday she could come again—

There was a tall blue jar filled with honeysuckle standing on the stone floor beside the door. Wincy breathed the sweet smell, thinking how it fitted with the lovely house.

Was it right, though, for her to be so happy, while her parents were grieving over Mark? They had urged her to accept Daphne's invitation, saying they would be out, too, since they were going to Evening Prayers. But was it right that she should have enjoyed her visit so much?

"You're coming too, aren't you?" Daphne asked, putting her arm through Wincy's and looking into her face hopefully.

Wincy did not want to go. But she would not refuse Daphne. She went along, sitting beside her new friend in the Warden's pew.

The windows of the old Chapel were boarded up and there were sandbags against the thick stone walls, yet the place was more beautiful than Wincy remembered. When the choir came streaming in, the little boys looked quite different with their surplices and solemn faces.

Wincy got to her feet under her own steam, no longer prodded by Nannie's possessive ghost. During the prayers she peeped between her fingers at the Warden and Daddy and Doctor Quelch sitting with other dignitaries in the great carved stalls of the choir. Across the aisle, she could see her mother and Angus. As Angus bent his downy head, an impressive collar popped out at the back of his coat.

Where had he got that collar? Had Mummie picked it up through the Barter Book at the Clothing Exchange? Or had it been stored in the boxroom for years and years, ever since Mark was nine? Mark . . .

Wincy shut her eyes and swallowed hard. Was he safe? But nobody was safe, really. A bomb might fall on the Chapel right now, killing them all. She hadn't realized all this in Belmont. Her mind knew it, but she hadn't felt the danger deep within, the way she did now.

If she were still in Belmont and the news about Mark had come to her in a letter, she would not be feeling it in this deep, real way. It would be more like something that happened to someone else in a book, or on the stage, not something that concerned her intimately. Life seemed to be largely a question of geography. If you were in the place where a bomb, or bad news happened to strike, it hit you. And if you chanced to be somewhere else, you got off free.

As she opened her eyes again, Wincy saw her mother grasping the back of the pew in front, her head bent over her hands. Her golden hair looked beautiful, even with that Oxford hat over it, but there was a forlorn curve to her shoulders, as though she were pressing her elbows against her ribs to hold in her sorrow. She must be praying for Mark.

But Wincy felt too old to pray. When you were little, you begged for things. But to a grown-up, that didn't seem the way to do.

Yet, the Chapel was filled with grown people—members of the College, many of them in military uniform, Doctor Quelch in his gown and Mrs. Quelch, looking like a large mother-cat with Brenda close beside her. They were all praying, or seeming to. There must be something to it which Wincy didn't understand. Nannie had never gone in for theology. She had been satisfied with the recitation of words. Some day, when she knew her better, Wincy would ask Daphne. . . .

During the lesson, Wincy found that Mrs. Quelch was looking at her, very distastefully, Wincy thought. She wondered where Francis was. Perhaps church bored him, too.

But really it hadn't been boring at all. It had been lovely and peaceful, and now it was already over, though it seemed it had hardly begun. What had she been thinking about that the time had gone so quickly?

Professor Turner fumbled with his gown as he rose from the choir-stall, steadying himself against the great carved arm. He seemed to have trouble getting to his feet, as though his knees were stiff. Wincy thought of his shrunken face when the news came about Mark. The shock had suddenly made him old.

The choir went out singing "God Moves in a Mysterious Way." Wincy recognized it as her father's favourite hymn. Before she knew it, she found herself in the porch beside Daphne, shaking hands with the Warden.

From his great height, he smiled at her, looking more like a baby than ever in his white surplice. Then he bent down and put his face close to Wincy's ear. "I'm still cogitating, Winifred," he whispered, "seeking something that will distract them—something gay, yet not frivolous, something engrossing—"

Daphne, standing close, heard the words too, and smiled at Wincy. The three of them shared a secret. They were like conspirators. . . .

"*Good* afternoon, Mrs. Quelch," Wincy heard the Warden saying, as he straightened and turned away from her. "And how are *you*, my dear?" he asked, reaching behind Mrs. Quelch to shake hands with Brenda.

But Mrs. Quelch gave the dear old gentleman only the most cursory greeting. She was glaring at Wincy. Clearly, she did not like seeing her standing there with the Godstows, conspiring. Wincy didn't know why Picklepuss should mind, but she obviously did.

"Everything I do gets me in wrong with Picklepuss," Wincy observed, as she and Daphne went out of the church. "Just going to Evening Prayers—"

"With whom?" Daphne asked, and Wincy jumped.

She had not meant to say this aloud. "Mrs. Quelch," she

explained primly. There was no harm in Daphne knowing that Mrs. Quelch disliked her, but she did hope she hadn't heard the name Angus had given the creature.

"I knew whom you meant," Daphne said, "but what was that amusing name you gave her?"

Wincy felt troubled. "Picklepuss," she repeated. "Sorry— it isn't very nice. People say it a lot in America. It means gherkin-face—you know, sour."

"Very fitting indeed!" Daphne exclaimed, laughing and laughing. "I must tell Daddy—he'll enjoy it."

"Oh, Daphne, *please* don't," Wincy begged. Then, as she thought of the Warden's gentle humour and the inscription on the lamp of his bicycle, she knew he would understand a joke. He was very old, and yet, oddly enough, he was far less likely to be shocked than her father.

Funny, Wincy thought, as she walked home, that some-thing dreadful should cause something lovely to happen. If it hadn't been for the bad news about Mark, the Warden and Daphne would never have come to call and we might not have met. . . .

It was true what the hymn said: *God moves in a mysterious way*. If only He would move for Mark—

XV

On the Monday, Wincy woke with what felt like a knot being twisted in her vitals. She dreaded going to school. New-fields always seemed to her like a tug-of-war, with the mistresses and all the girls on one end and Wincy on the other. Today she had an added fear. Suppose someone should say something to her about Mark? She wouldn't be able to bear it if anyone so much as mentioned his name. . . .

When she went down, she could hear the feeble wireless. Professor and Mrs. Turner were huddled over it, but when Mrs. Turner heard the sound of Wincy's step on the stairs, she mistook it for someone outside. She rushed to the door in hopes that there might be a messenger with news of Mark's safety. Unbearable strain was in her face as she turned back from the door in disappointment.

Tighter, tighter Wincy felt the knot twisting. In sudden urgency she ran upstairs again and was sick. When Hank had used the word the day he came to see her, she had laughed at him, but when it happened to you, it was no joke. Now she would be late for school. . . .

There was a fine cool drizzle when Wincy finally left the house. The geraniums and snapdragons glistened with it and the garden-walls had dark, wet patches, where they were not covered by roses. This was not at all the sort of weather Wincy had expected in June. In Belmont, they had always had a heat-wave at this time of the year.

The damp freshness, sharpening the smell of the grass and flowers, made Wincy feel a great deal better. But it must be very late, she knew, for there were no Newfields girls walking along in the little cotton print frocks, all exactly alike, which they wore in place of the serge tunics, now that summer had come.

The days were as deadly for Wincy as she had foreseen when she was sent to school a month ago: school, prep, and bedtime, with nothing but fiddling to break the monotony. Only the time she had spent yesterday with Daphne Godstow had been happy. That happiness lay warm about her, and yet it could not insulate her from the cold fear in the house and the dread of school.

She was late, and what would Miss Pusey say? At Agassiz, a kid would have explained that there was trouble at home and she would certainly have been excused. But Wincy didn't think you could talk about your troubles that way in England.

No one was in the corridors as Wincy hurried to her schoolroom—that was one good thing. But at the door, her hand on the knob and one foot already raised to walk in, she stopped. She simply couldn't—

Other days, she had managed to stick it—the stares, the faces some of the girls made at her long bob, the way they laughed when she pronounced a word the American way by mistake. Wincy didn't know half the things they were studying and none of the history, but Miss Pusey didn't seem to care. Even though she seemed to be doing very well in math—Euclid was what they called geometry here—she was beginning to fear that she might have to repeat the term if she didn't catch on to the other things very soon.

There was a clique which always referred to her as the "Yankee." One girl had come right out and said that Wincy had run away as soon as the going got bad in England. She hadn't put it that way, though. Wincy wouldn't even let herself think of what she had said. As though she had been given a say in the evacuation idea—she hadn't even known about it until almost the last minute, when she and Angus were bundled off to the boat.

When you were seasick, it never happened just once. You felt so much better after the first bout that you were sure it wasn't going to happen again. But after a little while, it always did.

Already the knot was beginning to tighten in Wincy's stomach as it had done before. Now she was late. Miss Pusey would be furious and Brenda and her friends would stare their cold stare.

But she couldn't remain in the corridor. . . . Swallowing hard, she opened the door. She went in . . .

The form was reciting. Wincy didn't dare raise her eyes as she slipped into her place. Yet she couldn't resist looking up a little speck when she had settled in.

Pusey was looking at her, but she wasn't furious. She actually gave Wincy a nod, nothing more than a ripple of her shingled hair to show she noticed Wincy, but it was friendly. It made Wincy feel better.

Did Pusey know about Mark? If only she wouldn't speak about him in front of everyone— Wincy knew she wouldn't be able to bear it. How could Pusey have found out? Was it in the paper?

Wincy's stomach began bouncing again. She shut her eyes. She could see the printed words as they would look, black against the grey paper of the *Times*: **TURNER, FLT. LT. J.M.S.** . . .

Picturing the words only made the knot bigger in her stomach. Tighter and tighter it was drawn as the words flickered before her. Wincy tried thinking of something else—her room in Belmont with the rambler roses running straight up the wallpaper. She could even see the way the roses slanted on the sides of the dormer windows. She tried thinking of Agassiz, of Mr. Thurman reciting Browning and all the kids rushing out at recess to play kick-the-can. The trouble within eased a trifle. Then Miss Pusey's voice broke across the happy picture. Wincy's stomach bounced again as she heard the mistress asking history questions.

At the close of school, she hurried home before anyone could say things to her about Mark. The rain had stopped. Everything looked cheerful, but now that she remembered about Mark again, there was a dull weight in her stomach where the knot had been before.

She had almost reached the garden-gate when she saw her father coming toward her from St. Giles. He biked slowly, with an effort. As each knee came up, it looked as if it could never gather the strength to push down again.

Wincy ran to meet her father and he handed her a gramophone record.

"A present," he said briefly, giving up the struggle to pedal and walking the rest of the way beside Wincy.

No sooner had they got to the house than Wincy hunted for the title of the record. It was *Pomp and Circumstance*.

"That's nice," Mrs. Turner said in a listless tone when Wincy showed it to her. "We really ought to have music for the children, John."

"Thank you, Daddy," Wincy said, giving Professor Turner a kiss.

"Are you pleased?" he asked hopefully. "I wasn't quite sure what sort of composer you would prefer, but I knew I couldn't go wrong with Sir Edward."

"It'll make a start," Wincy answered, trying to sound enthusiastic. "We must get Bach and Beethoven and Prokofieff. But what'll we play them on?"

"There's a gramophone in the nursery," Mrs. Turner reminded Wincy. "Nannie used to play it for you."

" 'Oranges and Lemons,' " Wincy said, remembering, "and 'My Lady Wind.' They were nice."

"Where's Angus?" the Professor inquired. "I have something for him, too."

"Upstairs," Mrs. Turner answered wearily. Life had become almost too much for her. Her two sons, who had never before given her acute concern—Nannie always having done the necessary—each in his own way had become cause for worry. There was a smudge of bathbrick across her cheek, and her hair, which was always so beautifully brushed, hung around her face in wisps. Wincy had never seen her mother look so hopeless.

"I'll get Angus," she offered, and started up.

"No," her mother said, restraining Wincy on the third step. "He's in disgrace."

"Why?" Professor Turner asked, turning toward his wife, as he hung his mackintosh on one of the branching arms.

Mrs. Turner sat down on the monk's bench. She looked so troubled and depressed, Wincy wanted to put her arms about her for comfort.

"I was polishing Mark's christening bowl and napkin-ring," Mrs. Turner said sadly, looking off into space. "The house was very quiet and I was thinking about—well, I was thinking. All at once, the most macabre laugh rent the air—macabre, John. No other word describes it."

"Bless me— What was it?"

"Angus," Mrs. Turner replied. " *'Who knows what evil lurks in the hearts of men?'* he muttered in a deep, menacing voice. He was quite alone there, in the dining room, but he answered himself, *'The Shadow knows.'* Then he laughed

again the same way—'nee-ah-ah-ah-ah-h-h.' The gruesome
tone upset me—such horrid implications."

Professor Turner put his arm about his wife and smoothed
her hair.

"Calm yourself, my dear," he said tranquilly. "We must
not become unreasonable in our hour of distress. No doubt
this is another of those American things."

"I dare say. But when I asked him, all he would answer was
'blue coal,' " Mrs. Turner said. "I was certain he was being
rude—pulling my leg, you know, with something ridiculous
like blue coal—although," she added vaguely, "in America
coal might even be blue. Nothing in the least would surprise
me about that country any more."

Wincy, still on the stairs, looked over the banister. "It's
only one of those radio programs he and Sutty used to listen
to, Mummie."

She did wish she could think of some way to cheer her
parents. This constant running to the door when there was a
sound in the road was becoming more than Wincy could
bear. If only a messenger might come with something definite.
It would be almost better knowing that Mark was dead than
not knowing anything.

No, Wincy said, giving herself a shake, no, I didn't mean
that, I didn't! Suppose it were Hank?

"A radio program? I see," Mrs. Turner said wearily. "It
did seem strange."

Professor Turner took a book out of his mack pocket.

"What have you got?" his wife asked.

"Wait and see," he replied, "the very thing for Angus."
In order to make the book seem like a present, he had
wrapped it up in his newspaper.

It was nice of him, Wincy thought, bringing them presents, when he was so frightfully distressed about Mark. She remembered what he had said the day she went to see him in his study: that he wished he had been more companionable with his elder son.

She wondered what he had chosen for Angus. There had been jolly books in her childhood—*Pip and Squeak, Playbox Annual, Tiger Tim*. Angus was just the right age for them, though they might seem a little tame after the comics in the *Boston Globe*.

"There's really no occasion for a present," Mrs. Turner said, leading the way to the drawing room. "Actually, Angus is doing very poorly in school. Last week Mr. Rottingdean said—"

"Daddy's present will make up to him for what old Rotter said," Wincy put in quickly. "It's not Angus's fault that he doesn't know Latin, and we mustn't let him take Rotter's criticism too seriously—we don't want him to get an inferiority complex."

"A *what*?" Mrs. Turner asked.

"An inferiority complex. Aunt Polly used to say—"

"Aunt Polly," Mrs. Turner repeated crossly. "Why didn't *she* see to it that Angus did his work properly? She spoiled the children, John, letting them choose their studies, playing with them, catering to them. It's 'Aunt Polly said this' and 'Aunt Polly did that' till I'm fed up."

"Rachel—you forget yourself. The Hilliards did their best for the children."

"Of course," Mrs. Turner said penitently. "I oughtn't to have said that. It was very good of them to take the children in—all unknown, and so on. . . ."

"You're upset, my dear," her husband said soothingly.

Mrs. Turner crumpled in her chair. "I expect you're right," she said bleakly. "It's awful—not knowing about Mark. Three days now— Oh, John, how can we go on this way, not knowing, perhaps, until the very end of the war. . . ."

"We do know, my dear," the Professor said in that calm voice of his, and even Wincy felt reassured by it. "There isn't any doubt but that he's safe somewhere. Not for an instant must we envisage anything else. He merely cannot communicate with us for the moment."

"Are you certain, John? If that's the case— Still, I do think Mrs. Hilliard made things difficult for us."

Wincy's cheeks felt hot. She knew her mother did not mean half the things she said, that she had simply lost control of herself. But Wincy felt embarrassed, as if, by listening to her mother, she was somehow disloyal to Aunt Polly.

"And that other thing," Mrs. Turner went on in a low voice, addressing her husband. "I confess, I cannot cope with the washing any more."

"Doesn't Angus do it himself?" Professor Turner asked. "It seems to me I've seen him at it."

"He does," Mrs. Turner conceded, "but in this wet weather we've difficulty airing linen. It's not as though we'd all the fires we used to have."

Professor Turner said, "I believe Wincy is right. This present will help Angus. One has to use psychology in matters of this sort."

Well I never, Wincy thought, looking at her father in astonishment.

"You've two books," she said in surprise, as she watched him empty his pockets.

"Yes, one of them is for myself. I noticed it when I was buying Angus his present at Blackwell's. As a matter of fact, Wincy," he said, "it's something to do with psychology. You have piqued my curiosity—my intellectual curiosity."

Wincy took the book and looked at it.

"Treatise on psychology by a Cambridge don," the Professor explained. "I confess, it sounds like some sort of mechanical treatise—projections, reflexes, mechanisms, conditions—nothing at all to do with the mind. But I only glanced briefly at it in the shop."

"By the by," Mrs. Turner said, "Quelch telephoned. The Warden wishes to see you tonight about this Undergraduate Approach."

Professor Turner's face fell.

"Again?" he asked in disappointment. "Bother! I had looked forward to reading the book."

"May I call Angus now?" Wincy asked.

"Yes," Mrs. Turner said. "John," she added, her face brightening, "we'll put the present on the mantelpiece and let Angus *look* at it—a reward he is to receive when he has passed a dry night."

Wincy called Angus down and brought him into the drawing room. Although she had told him that there was a present for him, he looked dejected. It was a shame the way all the bounce had gone out of him since he heard he was going to be sent to boarding-school.

But when he saw the parcel on the mantelpiece, his face brightened.

"Gee, Dad, thanks," he exclaimed. "Gee, that's swell!"

Professor Turner glanced at his wife a little sheepishly.

Then he took the parcel off the mantelpiece and placed it in his son's hand.

Wincy wondered which was the more eager—Angus or his father—as the parcel was opened. The book had a grey cover, stamped with a picture of Jason holding the Golden Fleece.

Angus read the title-page. *The Age of Fable*, by Thomas Bulfinch. "Oh," he sighed, skimming through the pages, his face and voice falling, "construe. . . ." He laid the book down and went to the window, looking out while he fiddled with the weight at the end of the curtain-cord.

Wincy felt sorry for her father. "I'll read it with you, Angus," she said brightly. "It's going to be fun."

"Okay," Angus answered without enthusiasm. Then his tone became urgent, "Daddy, why can't I stay at St. George's next term? Tons of the chaps in my form are going to be there."

"You must leave it to your elders to decide upon your education, my boy," Professor Turner answered gently. His face was very white and drawn. For all that outward calm, he was as troubled as his wife.

If only the Warden could find some way of helping her parents, Wincy thought. He had said he was cogitating—the word amused her faintly.

Mrs. Turner went to the window and put a hand on Angus' shoulder. "I'm sorry I was cross, darling," she said. "You see, I'm just a wee bit nervy today and I didn't know about the 'Shadow'. But Wincy told me you and Sutty used to listen to it on the wireless."

Angus forgot his troubles. "Boy, oh boy," he exclaimed, his face lighting at the memory, "were we scared—" Then he added, as he relived the thrill of horror, "and did we love it?"

"I can't answer your question," Mrs. Turner said earnestly, "since I wasn't there, but I gather you did." She ran her fingers affectionately through Angus's hair. "You'll like St. Tim's, darling—once you become accustomed to it."

The happy light faded from Angus's face. "Well, if I've got to go away," he said with a sigh, "I'm going back to Agassiz. Sutty and Uncle Bill will be ever so pleased." His voice grew dreamy. "I can't think how Aunt Polly gets along without me, anyhow."

There was a terrible silence.

"Rachel," Professor Turner suddenly said in a hearty voice, as if he had not heard the last remark, "when are we going to have our tea? Angus and I feel no end peckish."

XVI

DURING THE night, Warden Godstow had an inspiration. He lay in his bed in the ancient house at the bottom of the College Gardens, watching moonlight streak the polished oak walls of his room.

Wincy was serving the porridge in the silent dining room five days after her parents received the sad news about Mark, when the telephone rang. As soon as Mrs. Turner heard the Warden's voice, she put her husband on the line.

"The Undergraduate Approach again, most likely," she whispered cynically.

It was not, however, Professor Turner whom the Warden wished to speak with, and he made that point so clear that the Professor was a trifle nettled.

"Not scheming to become a don, are you?" he asked Wincy superciliously, as she came to the telephone, and in his eagerness to discover what the Warden could possibly have to say to his daughter, he hovered near the instrument, letting his porridge grow cold.

Since Warden Godstow did all the talking, Professor Turner was unable to discover anything at all, except that Wincy was tremendously pleased.

"What about the score?" she asked.

"Ah, it's a tennis party," the Professor whispered, his curiosity relieved, " or a cricket match."

When the conversation was ended, Wincy would reveal nothing. "He has the most wonderful idea," was all she would say. "I'm not to tell you and Mummie—it's a surprise." She enjoyed the uncontrolled amazement in her father's face as she added casually, "They're coming round tonight, by the way—the Warden and Daphne."

"Coming to see us again?" he asked incredulously. "The Old Boy seldom goes visiting. It's quite an honour to have him, you know, these days." The Professor rushed into the dining room to tell his wife the news.

The Warden had been seeking some means of distracting the unhappy Turners while they waited for news of their missing son. And during the night the idea had come to him— he would persuade them to join in playing the *Toy Symphony*, of which Wincy had spoken. The Turners might not at first feel inclined to participate in such childish merriment, but in the end, the Warden felt sure, no one could resist the charm of that gay work, nor, while concentrating on its performance, brood over sorrow.

It would be relatively simple to collect some sort of instruments, but the printed score presented a problem, as Wincy pointed out, for it was a piece not often played, and even music-lovers would not be apt to have a copy of it in their library. The Warden had already discovered that it was not for sale at Acott's in Magdalen Street, but he assured Wincy that Mr. Bunter, the College librarian, would put his hand on a copy. There must be one somewhere in the University and he would see that they got it, even if they had to filch it from the Bodleian.

Wincy swallowed her porridge, already deciding the instrument each person should play. She saw the orchestra as it used to look in Belmont, the tiny toy instruments, the happy players lost in concentration—everyone making the most incredible racket, and loving it.

Angus alone shared the secret. He bustled about after tea, pushing the furniture back against the wall to make room for the dining room chairs. "We're fixing Oxford up good," he said happily. "Pretty soon we'll have it nearly as nice as Belmont."

It was wonderful to see Angus so happy. That boarding-school business—Wincy would not think of that, though, tonight. They were going to have a gay evening.

But Mrs. Turner was not cheered. She had grown silent after the outburst of the previous day. Yet that look of defeat lingered in her eyes. Nor did she rejoice particularly in the reorganization of her drawing room.

In the midst of all the preparations, Wincy stopped. Would the *Toy Symphony* really cheer her parents and take their minds off their grief? The Warden seemed to think so, but he didn't know them the way she did. Besides, though it might be a gay evening, it couldn't bring Mark back. She felt tired, suddenly.

Angus brought Professor Turner's reading-stand down from his study. Finding that it was about to fall apart, he tightened it up and placed it before the hearth.

"That's a swell idea," Wincy said, trying to show enthusiasm for Angus's sake. "I'd been wondering what I'd use for the score."

Angus was ranging the chairs in a semicircle facing the reading-stand. "You going to be the conductor?" he asked in surprise.

"I'm going to try," Wincy said faintly. "There's nobody else. The Warden can't read a score. We'll make him concert-master."

She had never tried conducting, but she supposed she could do it. She remembered how Uncle Bill had indicated the beats with his head as he played the fiddle . . . If only Uncle Bill could be here, the symphony would go so much better. If only Hank could be here—

Those funny sounds that used to jump out of his clarinet . . . Wincy smiled as she remembered. She chose the chair she would give him—there, on her right. She could almost see him in it, his long legs tucked under, his hair standing up stiff as a brush, and that new look about his eyes—

"You're not giving a concert party?" Professor Turner asked, and Wincy jumped. She had not heard him come home. "The Warden plays the flute, but only at home of late," the Professor explained.

The drawing room had loosened up wonderfully. Even the brown mantelshelf did not look quite so overpowering. The photographs of the Parthenon hanging above it had always annoyed Wincy because they were hung symmetrically. She felt certain that if they were taken down and replaced regardless of size, they would be more interesting. She had never dared make the change before, but now she tried it and the result was marvellous.

After supper, Mrs. Turner said she would do the blackout and prepare the coffee.

"Mind you make it like Wincy's, Rachel," the Professor warned. "None of that English ditch-water."

Angus brought the trumpet and drum he had played with as a little chap down from the nursery, as well as the nightingale, which Professor Hilliard had let him take home when he left Belmont. "What about the rattle?" he asked Wincy anxiously.

The score called for a rattle. In Belmont, they had used a wooden noise-maker, left over from a New Year's Eve party.

Professor Turner hovered in the passage, watching the preparations.

"Do you mean one of those things babies amuse themselves with?" he asked. "What ever can you want *that* for?"

"One of those would do," Angus replied, enjoying his father's curiosity.

"Why don't you ask Mrs. Palmer across the road?" the Professor suggested. "I expect she has a rattle for her baby."

Angus flew through the passage and out the door.

Mrs. Turner stood at the door, looking in. She tried hard to conceal her disapproval, but when Angus left the house, she could not help asking, "Does he really mean to use my cooking-pan lids in the drawing room? I can't think what he wants them for—with the Warden coming."

"I'm afraid we'll have to use them," Wincy said, "since we've no cymbals."

"And that dreadful nightingale—he drools so. I shan't want water spilled in the drawing room."

"Let him, Rachel," the Professor urged. "It seems to be a necessary adjunct to these mysterious rites. The thing I can't fathom is what the Old Boy can have to do with all this childish pother—one of the foremost philosophers of our time, too."

The bell clanged and Professor Turner went to open the door, stopping in the passage to straighten his scarf.

Mrs. Turner suddenly noticed the pictures of the Parthenon which Wincy had rearranged. "These don't belong this way," she said, hastily putting them back in their original order.

Only Francis and Brenda Quelch were at the door and the Professor's face showed disappointment, which he quickly concealed. But it did seem out of place, he whispered to Wincy, to have invited children with the Warden. She explained that she had asked them because two more players were needed.

"Then it must be charades," the Professor declared triumphantly.

The Godstows arrived at last, bringing their instruments and music-stands and the precious score. Then Angus came in with Baby Palmer's rattle. It was so different from the one the Hilliards had used that he kept shaking it to see whether it made enough sound.

"Do stop the din, Angus," Mrs. Turner begged, leading the way into her ravaged drawing room.

And now Professor Turner could no longer conceal his curiosity. He hopped about impatiently with his nose thrust forward.

Trying to smell out the secret, Wincy said to herself with a smile. Sometimes he's like Angus . . .

Daphne stood near the bow-window talking to Mrs. Turner. Wincy could only see the back of her head with the hair coiled about it, but Mrs. Turner looked over toward her in a way which gave Wincy the feeling that she was being discussed. She felt uneasy, wondering what they were saying. Then Mrs. Turner took on an expression of pleased surprise, smiling at Wincy across the room. Daphne must have said something very nice about her. She was happy.

The players began to take the seats that Wincy assigned to them. When everyone was settled, the Warden rose, his child-like face glowing with pleasure.

"Ladies and gentlemen," he said bowing deeply, "this evening we propose to bring back the spirit of the eighteenth century by playing Haydn's *Toy Symphony*. This work, while scored in part for toy instruments, is, nevertheless, a real symphony. To perform it is a rare privilege, for it takes a skilled conductor."

Everyone looked politely attentive, but Wincy noticed that Francis Quelch was really interested. She remembered how he had spoken to her about American swing bands at that fateful tea party. Perhaps he liked good music, too. She wished she knew him well enough to find out.

"When I discovered," the Warden was saying, "that we have a skilled conductor here in our very midst, I could not wait to assemble an orchestra. Mistress Winifred," he announced, drawing Wincy to the place before the hearth where the reading-stand stood with the score laid open, "will now wield the bâton and we shall be her faithful followers."

Wincy curtsied gravely.

Taking his seat, the Warden began to applaud so vigorously that the other players joined.

Wincy felt her cheeks grow hot, but she was pleased. A happy glow enveloped her as she and the Godstows tuned up. She had not heard any instrument but her own since leaving Belmont. The three instruments—flute, violin and 'cello—blended together, coming closer in pitch until they reached unison.

Wincy watched Daphne tune, turning the large pegs in her capable fingers as she bowed. When Daphne was satisfied, she looked up expectantly at Wincy. And Wincy felt suddenly important. She had never felt that way before in this room.

Angus bustled about busily, giving out the instruments and music. First he handed his father the toy trumpet.

" 'Of the harmonies I know nothing,' " Professor Turner protested and could not resist adding for his son's edification, "thus Socrates, Plato's *Republic*, Book Three."

"None for me, dear," Mrs. Turner said. "I'm not musical."

"That doesn't matter," Angus insisted. "You can't listen—the sound would kill you." He left the music with his mother.

Brenda looked frightened. "I've never played the cymbals," she said, almost in a whisper.

"I say," Francis objected, "I don't know a crotchet from a quaver."

"It doesn't matter," Wincy told everyone, from behind the reading-stand. "You don't have to know how to read music, but you must watch and count carefully. The Warden,

Daphne and I are going to play the melody on real instruments and you are going to play the accompaniment on toys.
Now I'll explain how it's done—"

"But I can't read a note of music," Mrs. Turner protested.

"Just wait, Mummie, and you'll see. I'm going to beat like
this," she indicated the rhythm in the air with her bow, just
as Uncle Bill used to do, "and you will count the measures
you rest until it's time for you to come in."

Without a doubt, everyone seemed interested, even her
parents, Wincy thought. There were a number of questions.
Finally the players began to understand what was expected
of them.

"Now we're ready to begin," Wincy said, "but first we'll
introduce the players and their instruments. Our concert-
master, playing the cuckoo—"

Warden Godstow rose, held up his flute, and made a deep
bow. He was simply bursting with pleasure.

"The Warden also plays the part of the quail in the *Trio*,"
Wincy added.

The Warden bowed again.

"Now the 'cello—you needn't hold *that* up," Wincy added,
laughing.

Daphne stood up and curtsied in an old-fashioned way.

"Now the rattle," Wincy announced, turning to her
mother.

Mrs. Turner rose, feeling slightly foolish, as she held up
Baby Palmer's rattle. Everyone laughed.

"Next, the cymbals," Wincy said. "As you see, we haven't
a real pair."

Brenda stood up, holding the saucepan-lids. She was both
pleased and frightened, keeping her eyes on the ground as she

curtsied. Everyone was amused to see that she was going to play her part with kitchen utensils.

"The trumpet and drum play in unison," Wincy announced, beckoning with her bow for Professor Turner and Francis to rise.

The toys from the nursery-cupboard looked comical in the hands of the two men and the orchestra laughed anew.

"Please blow, Daddy, so we can hear if you're in tune," Wincy said, plucking her A string.

A feeble peep emerged from the trumpet. The players roared.

"Louder, please," Wincy commanded with great dignity.

The Professor tried again. His face was pink. Although he was straining to bring out the tone, there were amused crinkles around his eyes.

"Well, it's not exactly in pitch," Wincy admitted, "but I expect it's the best we can do with that trumpet. Now the nightingale—"

Angus stood up and proudly displayed his instrument, dripping water all over the floor.

Everyone was particularly interested in the nightingale because it was really like the one Haydn had used. The guests watched Angus blow through the cup of water at the base of the little metal bird. The beak and tail vibrated.

"It sounds precisely like a nightingale," Daphne declared, enchanted with the warbling note.

" 'Hail to thee, blithe spirit,' " the Warden declaimed, leaning over and patting Angus on the shoulder, but Angus stared at him blankly.

"Last of all," Wincy said modestly, holding up the violin, "the fiddle. I'll beckon to each of you when it's your turn to come in, though you can tell for yourselves, if you count carefully. Now the tempo of the first movement is *Allegro* and goes like this—" she played the first few bars, Daphne joining in the bass.

Everyone was attentive. They sat erect, instruments poised, ready to start at the signal. Wincy opened the score.

"May I turn you over?" the Warden asked Wincy, jumping up gallantly.

Wincy looked at him in astonishment. Perhaps the old gentleman was going nuts in his old age. Then she realized that she had been taken in by the English idiom and burst out laughing.

"Thank you," she said, bending down a corner of the page, "I can turn for myself, I think."

The Warden sat down again and when Wincy saw that he had his flute ready she announced that they would begin. "I'll count one measure first and then you'll come in when I nod my head." She counted four beats, waving her bow, and the symphony began.

The violin and 'cello carried the melody along so well that even when some of the other instruments did not come in at the right time, the symphony proceeded.

"That's the cuckoo—" Mrs. Turner exclaimed in surprise, when the Warden played his thirds. "That's precisely the way it sounds on Boar's Hill."

At the end of the first few measures, Wincy rapped the reading-stand with her bow.

"Good—" she exclaimed, "everyone came in on time." The players laughed. "Well, nearly on time," Wincy admitted, laughing, too. "Francis, a little softer, please—you're drowning out the other instruments. And, Brenda, you must count more carefully."

Francis tapped the drum softly. Then he looked up questioningly at Wincy and she gave him a satisfied nod. She could see he was enjoying himself and she was pleased. She hadn't thought he cared for anything but punting.

"The Angel Gabriel," Warden Godstow exclaimed, leaning across to Professor Turner and pointing to the toy trumpet. "I had no notion you were a musician, Turner." He laughed.

The Professor said later that in all the years he had been at St. James's, he had never seen the Old Boy look so happy.

"Now," said Wincy, rapping for attention, "we'll start again. This time we'll try to go through the whole first movement."

In the *Trio* the Warden played the part of a quail instead of the cuckoo, and Wincy noticed the other players laugh when they recognized the bird-call.

In the *Finale* they made a magnificent noise: the violin and 'cello carried the melody, the trumpet and drum were going great guns and Brenda brought the saucepan-lids together smartly, while the Warden came in with the cuckoo again and Mrs. Turner trailed along, violently shaking her rattle. Angus had a pool of water at his feet.

There was a round of laughter as the last measure subsided.

"Splendid, my dear," the Warden exclaimed, patting Wincy's shoulder. "I think we've cheered them no end."

Wincy looked up from the score. What she saw startled her.

An airman in blue-grey stood in the doorway. Someone from St. James's, probably. No one could have heard the bell clang above the din of the *Finale* and perhaps Angus, coming in with the rattle, had left the door open. But how rude of a stranger to walk in like that . . .

Mrs. Turner was the first to notice Wincy's startled expression. Glancing over her shoulder, she jumped up and ran into the passage. "Mark!" she cried, "Mark, are you safe?"

In an instant, Professor Turner and Francis were on their feet.

"Mark!" everyone cried, "Mark!" The room echoed with the name.

Mark's parents clung to him, not quite daring to display their affection and emotion, yet not succeeding in concealing them, either. Although they were radiant, they looked almost as shocked as when the telegram arrived saying Mark was missing.

"Are you safe?" Mrs. Turner repeated anxiously, plucking at the sleeve of her son's uniform and looking him over from head to foot.

"Why didn't you let us know you were coming, my boy?" the Professor asked at the same moment.

"I did," Mark answered, ignoring his mother's question. He was obviously embarrassed.

Professor Turner looked puzzled. "We had only the one telegram saying—we didn't know—we thought—"

"But I sent one as soon as I could," Mark explained.

"It hasn't yet arrived," the Professor said, his face clearing. "In any case, it doesn't matter now. We're delighted to see you, my boy."

The Godstows and Brenda surged toward the passage. But Angus hung back, clinging shyly to Wincy. The two stayed on the edge of the group, staring at their brother.

He was very handsome, Wincy thought, in a distinctly British way. His bearing was more soldierly than Hank's, but Hank hadn't been a soldier very long. Mark was tall, too, and his blue eyes looking over the heads of his parents, darted restlessly across the drawing room.

Francis said nothing as he shook hands with Mark, but when the two boys faced one another, Wincy could see that a world of unspoken messages passed between them.

Then Mark looked about at everyone else. He greeted the Warden and Daphne politely and waved at Brenda, but he looked faintly bored by the welcome. This puzzled Wincy, for she thought, considering how worried they had all been before, they appeared far too casual now that he was actually here, and quite alive.

They ought to show Mark, she thought, how happy they are that he's come home. Too many people of good taste. . . . She went forward to give her brother a proper welcome.

"The children are here, Mark," Mrs. Turner said, seeing Wincy advance. "Wincy and Angus are home, you know—"

Wincy grasped Mark's hand in both of hers. She wanted him to know how happy *she* was.

"I say, Wincy," he said, holding his sister at arm's length, "you *are* impetuous. . . ."

He spoke jokingly, but now that she was closer, Wincy saw that Mark's cheeks were sunken and his eyelids twitched.

Angus still looked confused by the surprise. He stood surveying Mark, speechless. "Well," he exclaimed at last, in the loud voice which Mrs. Turner had just got toned down, "I'll be d——,"—He caught himself in time. "*My sizzling aunt—*"

XVII

"I say," Mark exclaimed, as he watched Professor Turner scoop boiled mutton and parsnips out of the pot the following day. "Things *have* changed here."

Wincy, taking her place at table, was studying the details of her brother's face—the hollows under his narrow cheek-bones, the pointed nose like Mummie's, the restless eyes darting about under twitching lids. They had always been such calm eyes. . . .

"Changed, Mark?" Mrs. Turner asked in surprise as she sat down to dinner. She was beautiful with happiness as she surveyed her family complete about her. "It's only that the children are with us again," she said. "Children make a vast change in a household."

"No, not that," Mark answered. "Everything's different."

"I don't know why you should think so, I'm sure," Mrs. Turner said sorrowfully. "I rather prided myself on keeping things exactly as they were so that home would look the same to you when you returned. Not a thing has been moved in your room."

"I mean," Mark explained in confusion, evidently unaccustomed to analysing his thoughts for the scrutiny of his parents, "I mean—the way you were all playing when I popped in last night. You never did such things when I was at home. And Father on active duty on the kitchen front. . . ."

"I've learned a great deal—" the Professor said proudly, "to be setter, retriever and what to do for dishpan-hands."

Mark laughed. "And fancy us being matey with the

Warden," he went on, shaking his head, apparently unable to believe that this could be.

"Well, perhaps it is different," Mrs. Turner admitted. "It must have happened gradually, for I wasn't aware of any change. I wonder what could have brought it about."

"Vast improvement," Mark said bluntly.

His mother looked pleased, yet faintly puzzled. "Change," she repeated vaguely, almost to herself. "To be sure, the war . . ."

Mark had offered very little explanation about himself. He had been forced down in the Channel and picked up some hours later unharmed. But it was several days before he was able to return to his base and there had been some official confusion about his whereabouts. Now he was on his way to an assignment in the west of England and had two days to spend at home.

Wincy was surprised to see her parents placidly accepting Mark's silence. Perhaps he'll thaw out later, she had thought the previous night.

But he never did. He had always been reserved with his parents and he wasn't going to begin telling them things now, on his short leave. The bare facts about the crash seemed to content his parents, but Wincy wondered what it felt like to fall into the Channel. Judging by the way Mark looked, it must have been pretty bad. Had his plane burned, the way you saw them in the newsreels, and did he fall from a great height? Was he floundering for hours in the icy water, or sighted right away? Wincy was dying to know everything, but it didn't seem wise to ask while her parents were present. Perhaps later, when they were alone . . .

"Angus, have we any of that maple syrup left that you

brought from the States?" Professor Turner asked. "You must flip some flapjacks for Mark tomorrow morning."

Instantly, Angus left his mutton to go into the larder and squint down the can that Uncle Bill had brought him from Vermont. When he returned to the table, there was no need to ask Angus how the syrup situation stood. It was quite apparent from his expression that there was no more.

However, Angus's spirits had risen overnight. He could not leave Mark for an instant. Here, at last, was someone who understood things—generators, propellers, transmitters, motors—just as people did in Belmont.

"Do you *like* American dishes, Father?" Mark was asking. "I mean—you never held with foreign food."

"D'you know, my boy," the Professor said, in a confiding tone, "in all the years that I studied the classics—wellnigh half a century—I longed to taste nectar and ambrosia, and at last I have done so. In America these go under the name of 'flapjacks and maple syrup,' but I am certain they are none other than the food the gods partook of."

Mark eyed his father with astonishment, but he was even more surprised when, at the close of the meal, Professor Turner went into the kitchen and fetched a tray.

He was just about to pile the dishes on the tray when he noticed the picture of the red setter that Angus had painted on it.

"Sorry," he exclaimed, taking it back to the kitchen and exchanging it for another tray. "I'm retriever this week. One has to watch out for these things, Mark. You see, Angus is the taskmaster in this house now. He fills up a form with our duties and posts it in the scullery each Monday. We observe it to the letter."

Mark pondered this for a moment. "Vast improvement over that filthy-tempered hag we used to have in the kitchen," he remarked finally.

"Come up to the nursery, Mark," Angus begged, when the dishes were done. "I'll show you my things."

Now, Wincy thought as Mark followed Angus, we'll have him to ourselves. He used to feel too superior to come to the nursery, but he sees that things are different. After all, he's only a speck older than Hank, and Hank thought it worth while to come all the way across England to visit Angus and me. Hank and I click. Surely Mark will like being friends with me. . . .

Mrs. Turner stood in the passage and watched her three young people mount the stairs. "Just like old times!" she exclaimed happily. "I do wish Nannie could see you. But she wouldn't appreciate even then how grown up you are. I myself can hardly believe it—" As they reached the nursery, Wincy could still hear her mother. "If only I hadn't that Army hostel to care for today—" she said. "I should so love to stop at home."

Professor Turner came out of his study as Angus went by.

"Why don't you and Mark make that model-plane you brought me from Belmont?" he asked. "Mark will know how to do it." He held out the unopened box and Angus took it gladly.

"Gee, Mark, wait till you see this—it's a swell one," Angus shouted, running along behind, two steps at a time.

"You never came up here before we went away, did you?" Wincy asked, when they were in the nursery.

"Great snakes, no," Mark exclaimed. "Too stuffy with Nannie."

"Did she try to boss you, too? Daddy says he lived in mortal terror of her."

"Father's too meek altogether," Mark grumbled.

"Being a Greek professor makes all the difference, don't you think?" Wincy remarked. "If only it were chemistry—"

"Stuffy," Mark muttered. "All dons are."

Angus put the dope, nose-block, and propeller aside and laid the intricately marked boards out on the dwarf table with the working-drawings. He hadn't looked so happy since he left Belmont.

Mark was very much interested. Wincy watched him study the drawings and give commands to Angus, who jumped to carry them out. When they knew each other a little better, she and Mark might become close like Hank and Sally Sutton. They would go about together and have a swell time. He was right in what he said—dons *were* stuffy, if you stopped to think of it.

"I wonder whether it's an inferiority complex," she said thoughtfully, "because dons are so helpless compared to tradesmen and farmers and people like that."

"Where did you pick that up?" Mark asked, looking at her in surprise. "Over in America?"

But Wincy did not notice his question. She was thinking of her father. "He might have an inferiority complex," she said. "Funny—I never thought of that. Mark, I do wish we could do something about Daddy. He's terribly worried."

Mark looked up in mild curiosity.

"The Undergraduate Approach," Wincy explained knowingly. She had no idea what this was, but she was certain Mark would understand.

"What *are* you babbling about?" he asked.

"St. James's—something to do with the undergraduates—their approach. Daddy's dreadfully worried."

Mark shook his head and looked baffled. But he was not really interested. He turned his attention to the model again for a few minutes and then he stood up, stretching.

"You're not going away?" Angus asked, deeply disappointed.

"Meeting a chum," Mark explained.

"Need you go?" Angus begged.

Wincy looked at Mark shrewdly. "Is it—" she hesitated, "Francis Quelch?"

"Matter of fact, it is," he said, eyeing her curiously. "Any concern of yours?"

"I just wondered whether you were going on the River with him," Wincy said. "He asked me once. Mummie wouldn't let me go—"

"Not potty about him, are you?" Mark asked.

"Goodness, no!" Wincy exclaimed. "Actually, I don't even like him at all. Haven't you ever noticed the way his nose is the exact same shape as his father's and Brenda's?"

"No, I hadn't," Mark answered crossly.

"It's not repulsive—the nose, I mean," Wincy said hastily, not meaning to seem rude about Mark's friend. "It's very handsome, in fact. Francis's father is going to be the new Warden—did you know?"

"Can't be bothered," Mark muttered indifferently. "Francis ought to join the Navy."

"We had a foster-cousin in America," Wincy said shyly. "He's in the Army. His name is Hank Sutton—Harley, really, but we call him Hank."

Mark looked unimpressed.

"He came to see us here," Angus put in eagerly, "before he was shipped out."

"Pity you weren't home," Wincy said thoughtfully.

"I say, Wincy," Mark exclaimed, "I had no idea you were such a woman. I pictured you still an insect with those jumping plaits you used to wear."

"So did Mummie," Wincy answered. "Ever since we came home I've been convincing her that I'm not a child. I'm fifteen, you know."

"Shouldn't think it would take much convincing," Mark said meaningly. He walked toward the nursery-door but stopped as he was about to go out. "Look here, Wincy," he said. "Francis is my friend. I won't hold with any cheek concerning him."

"Sorry. I didn't mean anything, Mark—really. He's all right, in a way. It's just—" She would have to tell him now. "It's just that I like Hank." So that he would understand, Wincy added, "Somehow American men suit me better."

Mark leaned against the doorjamb spinning a sixpence in the air thoughtfully. His eyelids were twitching horribly.

"Rot!" he muttered, and walked off.

XVIII

"Don't you think it a good plan?" Mrs. Turner asked.

"Mmm."

"Don't you think it a good plan?" she asked again. "John, I don't think you've heard a word I've been saying."

Professor Turner looked up from his book. It was rare that he was at home in the evening. Fully half his nights were spent fire-watching or at Home Guard and the time for a bit of a read was a luxury. As he looked up, awareness gradually came into his eyes.

"What plan, Rachel? Oh yes, the little Quelch—having her in to tea with her mother. Yes, I certainly should."

"If she saw more of Wincy, she might be more friendly toward her," Mrs. Turner said. "Wincy is having rather a thin time at school, I gather. There seems to be the feeling, because she was evacuated . . ." She could not make herself state the case.

"What did you say?" the Professor asked. "Tomorrow? Yes, that will suit me excellently, for I shan't be coming home to tea. I'm not frightfully keen about Monica Quelch, you know."

"You won't be in to tea?" Mrs. Turner asked in surprise.

"No, I'm dining in Hall. Undergraduate Approach—" her husband murmured, looking longingly at his book. "Must see the Warden." He gave up the struggle to concentrate on

166

his wife's remarks and abandoned himself happily to reading.

Wincy sat at the writing-table near the French windows, trying to think of something to say to Sally Sutton. She had told her about playing the *Toy Symphony* two weeks ago—how her parents had taken part in it with real enthusiasm, and how delighted the old Warden had been playing the cuckoo, how Mark had turned up at the close of the *Finale*. She had not mentioned Newfields. She didn't wish Sally to know that it was beastly.

"John, what *is* that book?" Mrs. Turner asked suddenly.

"From the College Library," her husband replied without looking up. "Bunter suggested it when I mentioned that psychology book I bought at Blackwell's."

"Psychology?" Mrs. Turner asked vaguely. "You sound like Wincy."

"Knowledgeable creature, isn't she?" her husband exclaimed, putting down his book and rubbing his eyes. "Fancy her knowing so much at fifteen—"

Mrs. Turner dropped her knitting in her lap and looked directly at her husband. "Far too much, John," she said vehemently. "I don't like it. It's not right that a girl her age should be so aware of the opposite sex. Why, even when I was eighteen—"

"Come, come, my dear," the Professor broke in impatiently, "You can't say how you would have been at Wincy's age if your mother hadn't repressed you."

"Do you really think it—" she hesitated, "normal?" Mrs. Turner asked.

The Professor laughed. "I'm afraid you've more to learn in some ways than Wincy, Rachel," he said gently. "You ought to read this book. It's about behaviour."

"How can that be interesting?" Mrs. Turner asked. "I mean—it's only what we were all taught by our nannies." She frowned. "Isn't this something American?"

The Professor made a gesture of impatience. "Now, Rachel, you mustn't entertain the notion that America is the only forward country. I never heard of behaviour because it was too far removed from my classical studies, but we have some very competent investigators in this country."

"Of course," Mrs. Turner said. "If it's really important, I've no doubt England—"

"This man Watson I'm reading about, though—I believe he is an American. It seems he put some snakes and toads and other reptiles in a room with newly born infants. The infants were not in the least frightened. He demonstrated that people are unafraid until taught fear. It is an interesting theory."

"But what a dangerous thing to do, John, with helpless infants."

"They were harmless reptiles, I'm sure, Rachel. Besides, certain risks must be sustained in the interest of science—"

Wincy looked up in surprise. Science! Her father looked very earnest.

"We've come quite off the subject," Mrs. Turner was saying. "I do feel sorry for Wincy not having any friends. That's why I'm asking Brenda."

Wincy was surprised to hear herself being discussed this way. Her parents had apparently forgotten that she was there. But if she were, for example, to clear her throat now, they would feel upset over having spoken that way in her presence. The best thing, she decided, was to appear engrossed in her letter-writing. It would spare them all embarrassment.

"It must be rather dull for Wincy here," her father was

saying, "after all the friends and parties and larking about she was accustomed to in Belmont."

Mrs. Turner nodded thoughtfully. "If only I had the time to be with her more," she said. "But the W.V.S. and the shopping seem to take all my time. Brenda Quelch would be just the friend for her. Do you remember how, when they were little, they used to—"

"But she doesn't seem to fancy Brenda now," the Professor broke in impatiently.

"That will pass when she knows her better. I'll ask her to tea. Besides," Mrs. Turner's voice became intense, "I should rather like Monica to see how well Wincy is shaping—a few American corners have been rubbed off."

"I never noticed any corners," the Professor murmured. "Some of these Americans are extremely knowledgeable. There was a visiting anthropologist at the High Table this noon—quite a clever chap. He talked about Indian tribes and their customs. Apparently, in some parts, the children do not belong to their parents, but to the tribe."

"I suppose the American people are largely influenced by the Indians," Mrs. Turned remarked.

"I think not, Rachel, but the result of the children belonging to the whole tribe is that there is no jealousy amongst parents, since the children belong to all of them."

"Jealousy amongst parents?" Mrs. Turner repeated in surprise.

"Yes," Professor Turner explained, "such as English people feel when their children compete unsuccessfully for scholarships and so on."

"But, John, gentlefolk are not jealous."

"They do not show jealousy, but we know that all of us

feel it occasionally. D'you know, Rachel," her husband confided, "I sometimes wonder whether Monica's preoccupa-
tion with Wincy's behaviour may not be due, in part, to
jealousy. I mean, Wincy is so much more vivid than that
mousey little Quelch child."

"Oh, I don't think that can be, John," Mrs. Turner said
with conviction. "She's been ever so solicitous about the
children all through their American stay, worrying lest they
fall in with unscrupulous people and be ill treated."

"Well, I'm not sure that she wasn't *hoping* something of
the sort might happen, merely because Brenda stopped at
home."

"I really can't believe it," Mrs. Turner said, a trifle hurt.
"Monica is trying to counsel me in handling Wincy because
she has had more experience. I think it horrid to suspect
people's good intentions."

Professor Turner began reading again. His wife took up
her knitting. The room was quiet. After a long while, the
Professor closed the book over his finger and stared into space.

"A penny for your thoughts, my dear," Mrs. Turner said,
gaily.

"This book is rather illuminating," her husband said. "It
explains a great many things. But I forget myself, my dear.
Where are the children?" He looked about, but did not notice
Wincy.

"John," Mrs. Turner broke in, putting down her knitting,
"I do wish you had never read any of those psychology books.
All you do nowadays is read them and think about them and
imagine things. It makes me feel no end queer, as though
things weren't at all what they seem."

Professor Turner looked at his wife tenderly. "It *is* queer, all this new knowledge, and quite upsetting," he said. "But whatever mutations it may presage in my outlook, my dear, one thing—my affection for you—will always remain steadfast."

Wincy wished now that she had left the room sooner. The back of her eyes prickled, though she didn't understand why.

Mrs. Turner moved closer to her husband, resting her hand on his arm. "John," she said in a tense voice, "I must tell you something."

The Professor looked up gravely.

"That morning a fortnight ago, after the telegram arrived, you know. I was so terrified, thinking the worst had happened to Mark, praying— I had forgotten all about the little ones. And then I came upon them huddled on the monk's bench, the way they used to sit waiting for Nannie to wheel the pram round—you know how sticky she used to be about their keeping their shoes clean."

"Yes, yes—adhere to the subject, my dear."

"It wasn't anything," Mrs. Turner said softly, "just that they were huddled there looking so mournful that I suddenly felt frightfully sorry for them. It was strange—Mark was the one I was grieving about really, but I felt more than anything sorry for the children. They looked different to me, somehow—more like persons than like children. Queer that grief—"

"Aristotelian catharsis," the Professor murmured, stroking his wife's arm. "Purgation through pity and fear—"

"Perhaps you don't understand," Mrs. Turner broke in hastily. It always made her impatient when her husband "came all over the classical don," as she called it. "When I saw them huddled there—"

Involuntarily, Wincy stirred.

Mrs. Turner looked up. "Wincy!" she cried.

The Professor turned around, aghast. "Have you been here all this time?"

Wincy turned from the writing-desk and faced her parents. "I was writing to Sally Sutton," she said in a small voice.

"Were you eavesdropping whilst we discussed these— these matters that are not for children?" Mrs. Turner asked

"I wasn't eavesdropping," Wincy argued, blinking to ease the sensation behind her eyes, "I just happened to be sitting here and you were so absorbed, you didn't notice."

Mrs. Turner looked weak. "I think I shall make myself a cup of tea," she said faintly, starting for the passage.

At the door she stopped, pondering. She stood there a moment, the light from the overhead lamp shining on her lovely golden hair. Her hand lay across her cheek and there was a look of reminiscence in her eyes, as if she had gone back in memory, years and years.

"D'you know," she said, presumably to her husband, but it was more as if she were talking to herself, "it may be all for the best, her knowing these things. Perhaps if I had understood at Wincy's age— Of course, it would have been impossible—dear Mother was such a typical Victorian. But I mean, one really feels that one is getting closer to life. . . ."

It wasn't very clear, just what she did mean, but Wincy felt a flutter in her chest, finding herself so close to her mother's secret thought, closer than she had ever been before. Her mother was trying, trying hard to see things.

Sure enough, if you thought of Grannie Buckingham—she had died when Wincy was quite a small girl, but she could just remember her prim face with the hair pulled back tightly under her bonnet, her boned collars and her little lace parasol—you could understand that Mummie . . . Still, she was trying to catch up now, she really was.

XIX

THERE WAS a shop in St. Giles where they sold stamps behind a little cage, and a pillar-box at the bottom of Banbury Road, but Wincy always made a special trip to the head post office when she sent a letter to America. It was silly, she knew, but she felt her American letters deserved extra care.

After school the following afternoon, she biked through the Cornmarket with Sally Sutton's letter and down St. Aldate's, looking across to Christ Church from the post office.

Before she went to Belmont, she had never noticed what a beautiful place Christ Church was, she had only thought of it as Alice's House.

She remembered walking along beside her father in her Liberty smock on the way to Evening Prayers. As they passed under Tom Tower, he would tell her about Lewis Carroll writing *Alice in Wonderland* here when he wasn't doing sums. Lewis Carroll was such a good man, he used to add, that he didn't even want the pictures for his book drawn on Sunday.

Her father called this college "The House," and Wincy smiled now as she remembered thinking that of course he must mean "Alice's House."

She went into the post office and slid her letter into the box.

Wouldn't it be wonderful, Wincy thought, if I could make myself small like Alice, slip into the box, and travel to Belmont in an envelope?

She wheeled her bike round and was surprised to see Tom Tower turned to gold in the afternoon sun. In twenty minutes Great Tom would strike four. Wincy considered stopping to hear him, but she had to get back, because Brenda and her mother were coming to tea.

Everything was ready. Wincy had set out the tea-things and the kettle before going out. She had even rearranged the pictures of the Parthenon again the way she liked them. They looked so much nicer when they were not symmetrically placed. Would her mother leave them alone this time? she wondered.

With everything ready for tea, Wincy could spare five minutes to bike down to the bottom of St. Aldate's and have a look at the River from Folly Bridge.

A pity, Wincy thought, when Mrs. Turner was exerting herself so much that she and Brenda didn't like each other—not that there was anything wrong with Brenda, exactly. She was decent enough—just dull.

Mrs. Turner was frightfully anxious to show Mrs. Quelch that Wincy was becoming civilized. That was the main thing. When Doctor Quelch became Warden of St. James's, it would be awkward if his wife didn't approve of a Fellow's family.

Personally, Wincy said to herself, I wish old Picklepuss would slip down a drainpipe. Still, if it's going to help Daddy, I guess I can be decent to her.

One bank of the River was lined with college barges, but

there were punts and rowboats drifting idly about. Wincy rested her bike against the railing, and, looking up the River, she thought how lovely it was compared to the Charles, although when she was in Cambridge she had loved the Charles, especially the view of Beacon Hill and the dome of the State House as you rode over the River on the subway. But there were no great buildings and factories and ugly smoke stacks on the Isis.

"Halloa, Wincy," someone said behind her.

Turning, she saw Francis.

Her surprise was embarrassing. Francis Quelch was the last person Wincy expected to see. She had been dreaming about the Charles River.

"Hi, Francis—" Wincy hoped she appeared nonchalant, instead of startled. "Going on the River?"

He looked sunburned and outdoorish, yet not very happy. Those awful Smalls, Wincy supposed. Still, if he spent his days punting instead of studying, what did he expect?

"Just been," he answered, "on my way home now—have to swot, you know."

Instead of going, though, he leaned beside her on the railing, looking down at the water.

"Nice the way the willows along the Meadow hang over the water's edge, isn't it?" he asked.

His face lighted happily now. Wincy noticed, as she had never done before, that his forehead was high and bony and his nose was nicely proportioned, like his father's and Brenda's.

The Quelch Nose, Wincy said to herself, just managing not to laugh aloud.

"The Isis is the jolliest part of the Thames," Francis was

saying. "In fact, I shouldn't wonder if it's the prettiest stretch of water anywhere in the world."

Wincy looked up at him. It seemed such an inane remark. But then, if she had not been evacuated, if she had not seen the Charles at night, with the line of lights stretched along the Boston shore— "One if by land and two if by sea"—or the Hudson River, with that huge Washington Bridge gracefully slung across it, she might also have taken it for granted that her little corner of the earth was loveliest.

"Well, I mean—" Francis went on, awkwardly, seeing the doubt in Wincy's face, "I haven't been about, like you, Wincy. Other places must be nice, too. But to me this is paradise."

"Paradisis," Wincy corrected, laughing.

He looked at her, charmed with the discovery.

"Paradoxford," he retorted quickly. "Paradoxford on the Paradisis." He was immensely pleased with their combined wit.

They laughed over the phrase a long time, repeating it over and over.

"I wish you could come punting with me some day," Francis said wistfully. "Through Iffley Lock to Sandford . . ." he murmured dreamily.

Dragonflies were darting over the surface of the water. They made the only visible movement in the July stillness. It was very hot, but it was not the heat of Boston.

"I'll come some day," she said, and her voice sounded firmer than she had expected. "Quite soon, in fact."

"Cheers!" Francis exclaimed, and Wincy jumped. That was what he had said that dreadful day, when she had promised to go, but had been obliged to stand him up.

She looked at him from the side of her eye. There was something about Francis that she had never noticed before, an individual selfness that was his, and belonged to no one else. Until this moment he had been a boy like the others who walked about Oxford in cricket-blazer and flannels, except that she knew him. Now there was that individual selfness, a personalness about him that she had never seen in any boy, not even the ones she had known well, like Sandy Whipple and Hank Sutton.

It was something to do with the fall of his sandy hair, like salt-marsh grasses around Scituate, when the wind blew over the inlets; and with his mouth, which was determined and good natured, both at once—a funny thing.

Wincy thought, it isn't his nice eyes or the handsome Quelch Nose which give him that special look, but the funny things about him—his forehead, his mouth which hasn't made up its mind yet whether to be good natured or firm, and the way his Adam's apple keeps bobbing up and down. The funny things are nice.

A punt was making for the Bridge. First only a bit of it showed under the overhanging trees, but the man in the stern pushed out toward the middle of the River as he headed for the landing-stage. He was a middle-aged man—almost thirtyish—with long, powerful arms, and a look, Wincy thought, of easy strength, as he stood up in the boat. A woman wrapped in a shawl sat at his feet with a tea-basket beside her and her arms full of flowers.

"Some don and his wife, I expect," Francis said, following Wincy's eyes. "Been picking flowers near Iffley."

"They remind me of my foster-parents," Wincy said.

"They always seemed to go along like that—without fuss or bother. Wherever they went, they had flowers and food."

"Sounds jolly," Francis said. "You know, the way you tell about them, I can almost see those people."

He was the most *understanding* person. First, when she called Angus a bum at the tea party, he had passed over the incident as though he had been an American. Then, when her mother shamed her by sending him away, he had let that pass, too. No matter what mess there was, he always returned cheerful and friendly, as if nothing had happened at all. And now, here he was, understanding about the Hilliards as no one else in Oxford had done.

She hadn't seen all this in him before, any more than she had seen his face—really—until today, though she only glanced at it warily from the side of her eye while she pretended to be looking at the River. It was a moment of special seeing. That was a funny way to put it—it was an important moment, one of those things that stood out in history, like the day she arrived in Belmont, and that other day, two months ago, when she stepped out of the train in Oxford and found her parents waiting on the platform. Yes, an important moment.

Not really, for nothing had happened. She had simply biked down to the post office to mail a letter. She had gone to have a look at the River, and she had met Francis. But this moment felt so deeply special that she was certain when anything happened, she would always say to herself: that was the day after I met Francis on Folly Bridge, or that was a week after—a month, years, maybe—but she would always date events from this moment.

Everything felt different, looked different—Francis, the

couple in the punt, through whom she could see the Hilliards in Belmont, the Isis, which was her special River now, just as it was Francis's—there was a realness to things that had never been before.

"It was nice," Wincy said dreamily. "In the spring, all the kids in the neighbourhood used to come and play baseball in our backyard. Uncle Bill played with us when he was home —even Aunt Polly did sometimes.

"Sounds jolly—" Francis exclaimed. "Fancy Father—and *Mother*—" he grinned.

"Of course, our parents couldn't, with Home Guard and fire-watching and W.V.S.—it's different for them," Wincy said loyally. But she couldn't imagine Doctor and Mrs. Quelch being fun, not even in peacetime.

"I learned quite a good bit about baseball at a match I saw last autumn on the University athletic-ground," Francis said very seriously. "There was a chap explaining all the plays through a loudspeaker so the English people there would understand. There were some beautiful catches."

Wincy was still thinking of Belmont. "In summer," she continued, seeing it all again, "we used to go hosteling."

"Do you mean Youth Hostels? We have those."

"Yes. We'd all bike, except Aunt Polly. She followed in the station-wagon, because we used to go quite far sometimes and Angus couldn't make more than ten miles a day. Even Sutty got tired after fifteen. So Aunt Polly picked them up, put the bikes in the station-wagon, and we'd all meet at the next hostel."

"Sounds ever so jolly—" Francis put in.

"Of course," Wincy added, "Aunt Polly always took piles

of food and we'd cook the most heavenly suppers in the hostel kitchen. The Suttons used to come, too—you know, our foster-cousins."

"You mean that chap who came to see you?" Francis asked quickly, looking searchingly at Wincy. His Adam's apple was bobbing again. "Mother told me about it."

"Yes," Wincy answered vaguely.

When Francis mentioned Hank, she saw him again in his uniform, but only for an instant. It seemed a long time since he had come to Banbury Road.

Francis had gradually moved his hand down the railing. It barely touched Wincy's and she knew he wasn't going to move nearer. He was just companionably close.

"It was beastly with Mark away—until you came," he said suddenly, peering far up the River, as if trying to look around all the bends to Iffley.

Wincy couldn't imagine why his Adam's apple was so agitated, unless Francis also felt that this was an important moment.

The chimes of Great Tom floated down the Christ Church meadows and Wincy listened raptly, counting each stroke. There were six, yet the number held no meaning for Wincy. Standing on the bridge, she had seen new things in the world about her, but it was a timeless world. Six was not an hour, something with special meaning and exigencies—it was simply a rhythm.

Francis sighed. "I expect we'd better go," he said.

They started back across the Broad Walk, passing through the War Memorial gate. On the pavement Wincy noticed some copper letters and stopped to make them out in the dusky light.

"My sword," she read, "I give to him that shall succeed me in my pilgrimage."

Wincy looked up at Francis. He stood there, twiddling the grip of his handlebar and looking at the words on the ground like a dog that has been scolded. All the happiness was gone out of his face.

"I just can't stick it," he blurted out violently. "Hang it all, Wincy—a chap belongs on a ship, instead of swotting at construe."

My sword I give to him—so that was why Francis spent his days punting instead of studying—it was the closest to a ship that his father would let him get. Wincy saw now why Francis was having such a bad time. But why didn't he do something about it? If he was so determined to join the Navy, why didn't he?

"We have to make our own decisions, don't you think?" she said. "You can't expect the older generation to see things the way we do, at least, my family doesn't."

Francis looked up at Wincy in surprise. "Somehow I'd never thought of taking matters into my own hands. Perhaps I shall—how dim of me—"

"After all," Wincy went on, as they began biking again, "it's our world—the older generation is practically through with it."

They crossed Carfax and passed on through the Corn-market in silence. The streets were almost empty now, but Wincy did not notice. She was thinking how hard it is to do the right thing. You were supposed to obey your parents, yet they really were dumb—like the Quelches with Francis and her parents with Angus, wanting to send him away to school when anyone with the least knowledge of child psychology would know that was wrong.

And then, Mummie trying to make Wincy change her ways—ways she had learned from the Hilliards and knew to be good. It meant going back on the things you believed in, and no one could do that—not even for parents.

They were passing the Martyrs' Memorial now, biking along in happy silence through the evening haze. Suddenly Wincy knew she could never go back on the things that were right, even if it would make her a martyr. She hoped she wouldn't have to be a martyr, but—if it was inevitable—at least, she wouldn't have to put her right hand in the flame first.

"He must have wished that he had never taken back his word," Wincy said to Francis, "since he had to be burned anyway."

"Who?" Francis asked, surprised. His thought must have been a long way off. "Oh—Bishop Cranmer!" he exclaimed, nodding toward the monument. "I'd never thought of that. Beastly way to die—what?"

They parted at St. Giles Church with nothing but a look of farewell. It wasn't necessary to say anything, Wincy knew Francis felt the way she did about the important moment. As she turned into Banbury Road, she tried to see him riding up the Woodstock, but Francis had disappeared and there was an eerie loneliness in the empty streets.

Wincy pedalled hard now, standing up. She wanted to tell her mother about the happy afternoon—how different everything had become and how wonderful Francis really was, when you got to know him. Aunt Polly would have understood, but Aunt Polly wasn't her mother. You could share secrets like that better with your mother.

Wincy threw down her bike without bothering to ride it around to the shed. She rushed into the house. If only her mother hadn't gone out—now, while the wonderful feeling was still with her, she must tell her . . .

There was a light in the drawing room, and as Wincy hurried through the passage, she heard Mrs. Quelch's voice.

"I should call the police if I were you, Rachel," she was saying. "She may have run away. Such a strange child . . ."

For the first time since she slid Sally Sutton's letter into the box, Wincy remembered her mother's tea party.

It was almost two hours since she had met Francis on Folly Bridge.

XX

"WHERE HAVE you been, child?" Mrs. Turner cried, as Wincy stood in the passage. She drew her into the lighted drawing room, looking her over from head to foot. "Are you hurt, pet? I've been terrified."

Mrs. Quelch, sitting in the big arm-chair, looked Wincy over, too, but not with such solicitude. Brenda was not there and all signs of tea had been removed.

"So sorry," Wincy said breathlessly. "Am I late?"

"Late?" Mrs. Quelch echoed, sarcastically.

"I'm so relieved," Mrs. Turner said, still holding Wincy's hand. "I feared an accident. Where have you been?"

"Mailing a letter," Wincy said.

The pictures of the Parthenon still hung the way she had arranged them.

"It couldn't have taken two hours, just to the pillar-box, Wincy," Mrs. Turner said, but not reproachfully.

Wincy was surprised. She had done an awful thing—not turning up for tea when she was supposed to make a good impression on Picklepuss. Yet, Mrs. Turner was not even cross. She had often been upset over nothing. Now she merely looked relieved and loving, the way she had looked at the station when Wincy and Angus returned from America.

"I didn't think I was gone very long," Wincy murmured.

Had she and Francis spent nearly two hours on the bridge? Now that she was in bad again, she would never be able to tell her mother about the heavenly time she had had and all the odd things she discovered. Mrs. Turner would only be cross.

"Since Winifred is safe at home, Rachel," Mrs. Quelch announced, rising, "I shall go." She turned to Wincy, "I couldn't bear to leave your poor mother alone in her grief. So I sent Brenda home after tea to say that everything must proceed without me. Poor Francis has been at home all the afternoon swotting."

That's what you think, Picklepuss, Wincy thought.

"So good of you to remain," Mrs. Turner said, leading the way into the passage.

Picklepuss followed, but Wincy stayed behind. She was relieved to see the creature depart. Besides, she was starving, but there wasn't a thing to eat in sight and the kettle stood dead on the spirit-lamp.

"Fancy, almost three hours to the pillar-box," Mrs. Quelch murmured at the door-way, shaking her head at Wincy. "You didn't by any chance see a soldier on the way?" she added maliciously.

But Wincy did not notice the implications. The question had struck her as very funny, and in spite of the awfulness of the moment, she burst out laughing.

"No," she answered, "no, not a soldier, rather a sailor—well, not exactly—" She tried to find words that would accurately describe Francis's state of mind.

"I thought so—" Mrs. Quelch broke in triumphantly, without listening to all that Wincy had said. "You see Rachel, it was just as I feared. You wouldn't heed my predictions, but things like this happen to some young girls in wartime. It's the lure of the uniform." She shook her head sadly. "I'm so glad Brenda isn't that way," she added with nauseating smugness.

"He hasn't got a uniform, please," Wincy said. What would Mrs. Picklepuss say if she knew they were talking about her son?

"A sailor, yet not in uniform?" Mrs. Quelch said, irritably. "Rachel, the girl is either out of her senses or, worse, she is pulling my leg."

"Was it an American, Wincy?" Mrs. Turner asked.

"No, Mummie."

"Then it must have been a man you do not know, for you haven't met any British sailor since your return to Oxford—at least, not to my knowledge—not *properly*. Oh, Wincy, aren't you ashamed?"

"The town is full of strangers of all types," Mrs. Quelch said suspiciously. "What did he look like?"

Wincy hesitated a minute, picturing Francis again as he

had looked in that moment of special seeing on Folly Bridge.

"He has rather a boney forehead," she said, seeing Francis as he leaned against the railing, looking up toward Iffley, "and his mouth hasn't made up its mind yet whether to be good-natured or firm, but I *think* it's going to be firm. And his hair—his hair reminds me of the marsh grass around Scituate—that was where we used to go swimming in America—when the wind blew across the inlet. You'd know what I mean, if you could see Scituate."

Mrs. Turner looked at Wincy curiously. The anxiety had gone out of her face. "He sounds rather nice—" she murmured.

"Rachel," Mrs. Quelch broke in, interrupting Wincy's answer to her question. "I didn't say it before, although I've wanted to, ever since Winifred returned from that abominable country, and of course it's really no fault of hers, merely her misfortune in falling in with irresponsible people, but the child has positively been corrupted."

"Monica!"

"Yes, Rachel. I dare say you will understand when I say that—for the present, at least—I cannot let Brenda associate with Winifred. She simply must not see her. I have already forbidden Francis—"

"That's not in the least friendly, Monica."

"She has been running about town with a sailor," Mrs. Quelch said accusingly.

"I haven't," Wincy blurted out.

"You said you did."

"I didn't."

"Wincy, don't be rude to Mrs. Quelch."

"But I didn't."

"You did, Winifred," Mrs. Quelch said haughtily, "you are not only corrupt, but ill-mannered as well."

"But what you said wasn't true."

"Wincy," Mrs. Turner cried. "That's unpardonable rudeness. Apologize to Mrs. Quelch at once."

Wincy said nothing.

Mrs. Quelch moved into the passage. She looked toward the door, indicating that she was impatient to leave, but unable to do so before Wincy had made her apology.

But Wincy did not speak.

"Don't be stubborn, Wincy," Mrs. Turner pleaded.

"I can't apologize, Mummie," Wincy said, and she was terribly afraid that she was going to cry. "She wants me to admit something that isn't true."

"I think the child is perfectly right," Mrs. Turner said—Wincy could hardly believe it—"if she has not been running about with a sailor, there is nothing to apologize for."

"You, Rachel—you!" Mrs. Quelch shouted. "That foster-mother encouraged disrespect for English people in the girl, but you, Rachel—"

"Perhaps we do not understand her psychology," Mrs. Turner argued mildly.

"Mummie—"

"I never thought that you would uphold this wanton child," Mrs. Quelch said, really moving toward the door this time. "We all want to protect our children—that is one of the first rules of mothercraft—but we must not uphold them in sin."

"Monica, you have no right to speak about Wincy in such terms. I do believe you are envious because she has had such a happy experience abroad, whilst Brenda stopped at home with you."

Wincy was gloating. Her mother had told Picklepuss off, all right.

"I shall never forget this," Mrs. Quelch said menacingly, as she fumbled with the doorknob. "A disgrace to St. James's—"

All of a sudden, Mrs. Quelch changed shape before Wincy's eyes. She was no longer Picklepuss, or a charmed snake. She was the wife of the next Warden of St. James's, as powerful as she was mean. Once her husband became Warden, she would take out her spite on Professor Turner. And he, so helpless in the serene domain of antiquity, so unaware of the wicked world about him. . . .

"Mrs. Quelch," Wincy called, just as the door was about to be closed. "I didn't mean—"

—who near this spot yielded their bodies to be burned— Would she put her right hand in the flame first?

"I did mean it—I did mean every word."

The door slammed.

XXI

PROFESSOR TURNER had dined in Hall. He looked tremendously surprised when he opened the door on his return and found his wife and daughter sitting on the monk's bench in the passage.

"Uncommonly draughty place you've chosen to sit in, I should say, Rachel," he remarked, "though you look pleased as Punch. Mark's not getting a leave, by any chance?"

"No," said Mrs. Turner, "there's no word from Mark. Wincy and I simply collapsed here a few moments ago after demolishing Monica Quelch. We were exhausted, but victorious."

She smiled at Wincy. For the first time, they had fought on the same side. They had a fellow-feeling.

"Demolished her, did you?" the Professor asked, laughing.

"She was simply livid," Mrs. Turner replied gaily. "Come into the drawing room." She led the way and her husband followed.

But Wincy remained on the monk's bench for she felt superfluous. What is the world coming to? she asked herself, repressing a smile.

"Ever since Wincy returned," she could hear Mrs. Turner saying, "Monica has held such an unkind opinion of her."

Professor Turner looked up, surprised and angry.

"At first, I was rather inclined to agree with some of her criticism," Mrs. Turner admitted. "Wincy's foreign ways *were* very unsettling. The more Monica elaborated on them, the worse they seemed. But this afternoon she became insufferable, and I ticked her off."

"Ticked her off, eh?" the Professor repeated, laughing.

"She's no understanding of the child's psychology at all." Mrs. Turner complained.

Wincy jumped. Her mother—

"No what?" Professor Turner asked incredulously. "Bless my soul, Rachel. What happened then?"

"She went away, practically shaking her fist at me. Actually, Wincy *was* rather naughty," Mrs. Turner admitted, "coming home at half past six, when she knew we expected the Quelches for tea—"

"Where was she?" the Professor asked.

"Posting a letter."

"From tea-time till half past six? Impossible, Rachel."

"It did seem odd, but I was so relieved to find nothing un-toward had happened that I couldn't be cross, and then, when Monica implied such horrid things, I had to champion Wincy. For she hadn't done anything wrong—not morally wrong, you know. I was convinced of that—"

Wincy jumped off the monk's bench and ran into the drawing room. Impatience to share her secret with her mother rushed over her again.

"I met Francis," she explained. "I was just looking at the Isis and he happened along. We talked—I guess we must have talked a long time."

"You see, John," Mrs. Turner said happily, "I knew all along there was nothing to make such a to-do over. Wincy merely forgot to come home in time for tea. You won't do it again, will you, dear?" Suddenly she laughed. "Oh, Wincy, how funny—when she asked you what he looked like—it was her own boy, yet she never guessed."

Professor Turner seemed mystified by his wife's laughter, but it reassured him. "Poisonous, that woman," he declared. "I shouldn't heed a word she says—merely gossip."

"Yes, I'm afraid I've taken her too seriously altogether," his wife confessed.

"Seems to fancy herself an excellent helpmate, though," the Professor remarked. "Doing everything to secure Quelch the Wardenship—already rushing about pulling wires with the Fellows though the Old Boy won't resign for another three months."

"Do you really suppose that sort of thing will help her husband?" Mrs. Turner asked thoughtfully.

"No, I don't. But his wife must think so, or she wouldn't act the fool. No, Quelch will stand or fall on his merits—not his wife's intrigues—and his merits are considerable. I wish him well with all my heart, for he's a good man—quite the ablest scholar in his field."

"Yes, but as a warden—" Mrs. Turner began.

"That's it," the Professor broke in. "D'you know, Rachel, I sometimes wonder whether he really understands the minds of the men he tutors," the Professor confided.

"He's an able scholar—isn't that the main thing in a tutor?" Mrs. Turner asked.

"I used to think so, but actually, Rachel, I've come to realize just lately that it's not cramming matter into boys' heads that counts, but making the most of the equipment God has given them."

"I never thought of it that way."

"Neither did I, until just lately. And the curious thing is that I first saw this through studying the mind of a child— Angus. What a pity—I might have had this insight long ago, if I'd been closer to my children."

There was a pause. Professor and Mrs. Turner were engaged with their own thoughts. Though they said nothing, there was an intimacy in their silence which made Wincy feel superfluous again. She went back to the monk's bench in the passage.

"I fancy I've been a wee bit that way myself—about Wincy," Mrs. Turner said slowly, after a while. "I saw it this afternoon, when Monica was so abusive."

"A wee bit how?"

"I was interested in the mould and indifferent to the pudding."

The Professor smiled and put his arm about his wife.

"Rachel, speaking of food, *do* you think I might have some bread and jam? Beastly fare in Hall—shepherd's pie. I can't think why the steward doesn't do better. And the coffee! Now that I'm accustomed to Wincy's, I simply couldn't drink it."

They went into the kitchen. Wincy could no longer hear what her parents were saying. She felt out of things again, and she hadn't shared her secret, after all. Somehow, when it came to it, she wasn't able to tell about the important moment, when she had seen Francis in such a special way.

They wouldn't have understood. Only Francis could. She wanted to tell him all that had happened since they left each other at St. Giles Church—about Picklepuss, but of course she wouldn't say that that was what she called his mother—and how swell her mother had been to her and how she had already begun to measure time from that moment on Folly Bridge.

She wanted to tell him, she wanted to see him with a sharpness that startled her. It was within her, and yet all around her, like a thick wrapping, dividing her from the world without so completely that when she heard her name being whispered on the upper landing she jumped.

Angus had been sent to bed before Wincy reached home, but he sneaked down in the pyjamas which he was learning to wear and hung over the banister.

"I say, Wincy," he whispered. "Daddy let me come to his room at St. James's this afternoon. It's wizard."

"That's nice," Wincy said weakly, trying hard to look interested.

"There's a ripping little window called an oriel, and potty old gargoyles spitting water all around the building. He took me to the Library, too. You know what? The books are *chained* to the wall. Isn't that rum? Must be mostly gangsters in the College."

"Oh, no, Angus."

"Course," he added thoughtfully, leaning over still farther, "anyone with a hacksaw or an acetylene-torch could swipe them, anyway. And you know what he washes in?" Angus asked with such repressed excitement that Wincy was really anxious to know.

"The lav," she guessed.

"Nope. They don't have one. He has a little washstand thing in his office," Angus lingered emphatically over every word, "with brown doors around it, so it looks like the wall, and you can't tell what it is. When he opens it, there's a rack for his towels and a hook where he hangs his collar while he washes. It's much more fun than a bathroom."

Professor Turner came out of the kitchen munching his bread and jam. Wincy was afraid he would scold Angus and order him off to bed, but to her surprise he greeted him quite warmly and offered him a bite of his bread.

> "Musa, musae,
>   The gods were at tea.
>   Musae, musam,
>   Eating raspberry jam—"

he recited.

"Musa, musae, musae, musam," Angus repeated, cocking his head. "That's the first declension."

"Precisely," the Professor mumbled with his mouth full.

"Say it again, Daddy," Angus begged. "I'll remember it at school."

"I've been hearing about your wonderful room," Wincy said.

"Yes, we had a splendid time there, Angus and I," Professor Turner said. "Can't think why I never invited him before. I cherish that room in St. James's. Been in it, you know, ever since I first was made a Fellow—thirty-one years ago, come Michaelmas. But I never thought a child would be interested in the mouldering old place. Now up with you, Angus, and to bed."

"It's better than Uncle Bill's old lab," Angus called staunchly, as he mounted the stairs.

Uncle Bill's lab flashed before Wincy's mind, but it was a blurred picture, like a snapshot when the camera has moved. The details were in it, even Uncle Bill himself, with his tan lab coat and his crew-cut, but they were fuzzy and indistinct.

"If only I'd known," Professor Turner was saying, "I might have taken Mark, when he was a lad. Yes," he murmured, "thirty-one years. Couldn't bear to part with that room."

"Part with it? You mean lose your place in the College, Daddy?" Wincy cried.

And then she saw Mrs. Quelch again, but this was a very distinct picture. She was fumbling with the doorknob as she went out, roaring threats, like a cursing old witch. "A disgrace to St. James's," she had called Wincy. When her husband became Warden, she might even have Professor Turner expelled.

There was only one thing for Wincy to do. As she realized this, the tears she had managed to check while Mrs. Quelch was still there suddenly began running down her cheeks.

"Wincy—what is it?" Professor Turner asked in alarm, putting his arms about her. "What is it, chicken? Are you ill?"

Wincy couldn't tell him. It helped to feel her father's arms about her, but she knew that there was only one thing to do.

"Tell me, Wincy," he begged. "What is it?"

"I'll have to go back to Belmont," she sobbed. "Oh, Daddy —just when I was beginning to like it here."

"Beginning to like it here, are you? Well, I'm ever so pleased." He stroked her hair. "I was afraid you were find-ing it dull, after all the friends and parties and larking about that you were accustomed to in Belmont."

"You don't understand, Daddy," Wincy said, drying her eyes. "I've got to get away from here because of Mrs. Quelch."

"What's she to do with you, chicken? You've no need to bother with her. Poisonous woman—"

"You don't understand, Daddy."

"I do understand," he insisted. "I'm not quite such a relic of antiquity as you think me—as I was when you first came home, I should say. You have opened my eyes to a lot of things. And one of them is that the Quelches don't matter a fig—not a fig."

"But Daddy, when he's the Warden—"

The Professor made a gesture of impatience as he said, "It's not a question of being in the good graces of one's superior, my dear, but of doing one's job to the best of one's ability. 'Before virtue the gods have set toil,' Hesiod said."

"But if I remain in Oxford," Wincy said desperately, "Mrs. Quelch will get you expelled."

"Impossible!" the Professor exclaimed. "I've a University Chair, and in any case such action could only be taken by the Fellows of the College. Never fear—Quelch is an honest, upright man, though I don't fancy him as a Warden, I must say."

Mrs. Turner came in from the kitchen.

"Nonsense, Wincy," she said soothingly, stroking her daughter's head, "Monica was merely projecting her jealousy—"

"Rachel," the Professor began and then he hesitated. From force of habit, he mopped the bridge of his nose, but Wincy noticed that the beads of perspiration which usually appeared in stressful times were not there.

"Rachel, I wonder—do you suppose—could we have been a wee bit jealous of the Hilliards?"

Mrs. Turner went almost white. The sudden impact of her husband's question confused her and it was a long time before she could be certain of her answer.

"I shouldn't be surprised," she murmured slowly.

XXII

EVER SINCE Mark had been sent to the west of England, his parents no longer jumped up from the breakfast table when the post arrived. They worked as hard as ever before at their war jobs but appeared calm, even hopeful, as though possessed of an inner conviction that the worst of the war was over.

"If only people won't be too exhausted by the war to continue showing the same qualities of courage and comradeship when it is over," Professor Turner exclaimed at breakfast one morning a few weeks after Mrs. Quelch had been ticked off.

"Yes," Mrs. Turner said thoughtfully, "we shall need these qualities more than ever whilst we are returning to normal human relationships."

Angus brought in the post, devoured his porridge, and rushed off to play with the boy next door. He was cramming in all the fun he could get before going to boarding-school.

There was a letter for Wincy from Sally Sutton, full of her activities at Radcliffe College. She had taken part in a concert given by the Choral Society. She was majoring in biology. How did Wincy like her school?

School, Wincy thought impatiently. Who cares? Francis is the only subject I want to write Sally about. She's never met an English boy. It's going to be hard making her see how nice he is. . . .

197

But if she could tell Sally exactly how Francis had looked that afternoon on Folly Bridge, Sally would be able to picture him. She would understand why Wincy cared so much. . . .

"There's one for you, John, in Mrs. Hilliard's hand," Mrs. Turner remarked with surprise, looking over the remaining letters.

The Professor took it from her quickly, put it in his pocket, and tucked a napkin around the toast. He had begun to be quite fussy about having the toast hot.

His wife looked at him suspiciously. "How strange," she remarked slowly, "that the letter should be addressed to you. You never wrote to Mrs. Hilliard."

"I might have done," the Professor confessed, looking guilty.

"But you expressly asked me to write and thank her when the children returned," his wife said a bit reproachfully. "You said that sort of letter came best from the mother. . . ."

"So I did—when the children returned," Professor Turner admitted. "By the by, whom is your letter from?"

"Nannie," Mrs. Turner answered, looking at the handwriting. She opened the letter and read.

The saltmarsh grass, Wincy thought—Sally will know how his hair looks, because she has seen the wind blowing across the inlets near Scituate. But it isn't his hair I want her to see, it's him—he. That particular selfness . . .

"What does Nannie say?" Professor Turner asked before his wife had finished reading her letter. "Is she still in that Infant Welfare Centre in Birmingham?"

"Yes," Mrs. Turner answered, "but she's leaving shortly.

She doesn't say why. Oh, here it is—something to do with her age. John, she's coming back—how splendid!"

"What?" Wincy cried in alarm. "Nannie coming back?"

"Wouldn't it be rather awkward without maids?" the Professor asked.

"She says she'll give me a hand with the household," Mrs. Turner went on happily. "Isn't that splendid? Such a relief . . . but I wonder," she added, her voice becoming doubtful, "whether, with Angus away at school—"

Wincy jumped up from the table and moved toward her mother. "I'm too big for her," she stated in such a loud voice that she startled herself.   •

"Perhaps, Rachel," Professor Turner ventured, "perhaps, with Nannie to help you, we could keep Angus at home another year."

Wincy sent her father a grateful look.

"Such an excellent nurse." Mrs. Turner murmured, "Been with me ever since Mark was born."

"Age may be a criterion of quality in spirits," Professor Turner remarked whimsically, "but in a woman—"

His wife laughed. "Oh," she said, "we've quite forgotten your letter. Did you actually write to Mrs. Hilliard?"

Professor Turner had been thoughtfully munching his toast. "Those books we read together, you and I," he said after a pause, looking meaningly at his wife, "gave me many new thoughts—"

"That's just what I feared at the time," Mrs. Turner broke in. "Oh, John, they're not—" she could hardly get herself to speak the words, "Freudian thoughts?"

But Professor Turner did not hear the question. He was pondering something else. "Bless my soul, Rachel," he exclaimed, "with this new understanding of the mind, I believe I can even do something for young Quelch—prepare him for his Smalls."

"But you have done, John," Mrs. Turner put in. "I can't think how often that boy comes here to have a text explained, especially of late."

Wincy hadn't noticed Francis coming very often, either to have texts explained, or to see her. Why didn't he come? Was he swotting every minute? He had dropped in once or twice in the last month, but they had never really talked about anything important.

When her father spoke again, Wincy was startled. He and she had been thinking about the same person.

"He's a very intelligent boy, really—Francis Quelch," the Professor said. "Some psychological block must be the cause of his Latin difficulty. Rachel, I'm going to help that lad."

"Oh, Daddy, how wonderful—" Wincy exclaimed. All that swotting—if he failed . . .

"But what has all this to do with Mrs. Hilliard's letter?" Mrs. Turner asked suspiciously. "John, you are trying to evade the issue—did you write to her?"

"Somehow," the Professor admitted, "I suddenly appreciated how much the children's American stay had enriched them. You know, it might have been merely a regrettable hiatus in their life. I had to tell Mrs. Hilliard."

Mrs. Turner looked strangely at her husband, as if in many minds about what he had done. "Well," she said at length, "I can't think why you were secretive about it, but it was nice of you, writing her that. I've had much the same thought myself, of late."

"Besides," the Professor added, looking a little embar-

rassed, "I asked her to send me an American cookery-book."
He finished his toast with that slow calm which his wife
often found annoying. "I want to know how to make Boston
baked beans and brown bread."

Impatiently, Mrs. Turner watched him open the letter.
"Won't you read it to me?" she asked, as her husband turned
over the first page.

The Professor was so absorbed that instead of going back
to the beginning, he began reading aloud from the point
where he had been interrupted.

" 'How we do miss that pair!' " he read. " 'Of course we
knew, theoretically, that these pangs were in store for us, but
actually we feel the loss more than we had thought possible.
Things at every turn remind us of the happiness we had in
the years Wincy and Angus were with us.' "

Professor Turner looked up at his wife and the expression
in his eyes showed that he was deeply touched.

" 'Isn't it wonderful,' " he continued reading, " 'that children tend to remember the pleasant things and forget the
painful? From your letter I judge that Wincy and Angus
have painted a much rosier picture than we deserve—I know
there were times when humdrum household chores affected
my viewpoint to such an extent that I could have shaken each
of the three youngsters until his teeth rattled.' "

Mrs. Turner burst out laughing.

" 'Though I restrained myself,' " her husband went on,
turning the page, " 'I'm sure the children were aware of the
mental storm. But I'm glad that Wincy and Angus remember our merrier times rather than those moments when fatigue
made me act like the bad stepmother of fairybook tales.' "

Queer, Wincy thought, I don't seem to remember those

moments. "Bad stepmother" doesn't sound like Aunt Polly at all. It's more like Picklepuss.

Picklepuss—suddenly a thought flashed across Wincy's mind: maybe Picklepuss wouldn't let Francis come.

"So Mrs. Hilliard found the children tiresome, too, occasionally." Mrs. Turner exclaimed with satisfaction. "I never suspected. If I had known that, I should have been more kindly disposed toward her all along. I had the impression her household was always perfectly serene."

"Oh, no," Wincy put in, "not always. There was the time Angus almost set fire to the boxroom. And one New Year, when we all went away to Vermont for skiing, I forgot to leave the taps open in my bathroom and when we came home we found the pipes had burst."

"Dear me!" the Professor exclaimed.

"Poor woman," his wife murmured, smiling sympathetically, "with two strange infants—I, at any rate, had Nannie—"

"And how you wished for her when the children returned," her husband reminded her.

Yes, Francis probably didn't come because Picklepuss wouldn't let him, Wincy thought. She hadn't made a secret of her dislike for Wincy. Still, if he really cared, he would come anyhow—

"Nannie used to turn them out so beautifully," Mrs. Turner was saying, "white shoes and starched frocks. She's a treasure, but—" her voice trailed off uncertainly, "I'm not convinced that I want her back, John. She's very set, you know."

"Do I not?" Professor Turner replied quickly. "I used to live in mortal terror of her. I've wondered recently whether she didn't do the children more harm than good."

Mrs. Turner did not reply. She was looking out of the window thoughtfully.

Wincy was thoughtful, too. Perhaps it wasn't Picklepuss. Perhaps Francis didn't come because he felt like those pills at school who thought she ought not to have deserted England in her hour of need. If she only knew—

"Nannie could go to her married sister in Chipping Norton," Mrs. Turner said tentatively. There was another pause. "I don't believe I'll have her," she announced finally, great daring in her voice.

Wincy clutched her mother's arm. "Do let her come," she begged. It was her week to be retriever, but she had stood about with the tray and done nothing. If Nannie came, there might still be a chance for Angus to stay home.

"Poor woman," Mrs. Turner repeated, coming back to Mrs. Hilliard, "she had no help in the household either, and *three* young children."

Wincy glanced at the clock in the drawing room and was horrified to find that it was almost time for her music-lesson. "You will let Nannie come?" she asked urgently, piling plates on the tray in a rush. She did not dare leave before the matter was settled.

"Don't worry, chicken," Professor Turner said, as he helped Wincy remove the dishes, "I expect Angus will stop at home in any case—I simply couldn't get on without him."

"He does seem a little chap to be pushing off into the world alone," Mrs. Turner agreed. "I couldn't bear it, actually."

Wincy rushed off in a glow of happiness. Angus was safe. Life was wonderful, if only Francis . . .

Maybe, after all, he hadn't felt that that was an important

moment, there on Folly Bridge, yet the way his Adam's apple had bobbed up and down, she had thought—she would have to do something—explain that evacuation hadn't been her idea. But perhaps that wasn't the trouble at all. Perhaps—she didn't know.

Disconsolately, she fetched her violin and music. In the passage, Mrs. Turner's words were distinctly audible.

"I've been meaning to tell you, John, but I couldn't mention it in Wincy's presence: Angus's bed has been dry for the past fortnight."

"Has it really? Jolly good!" the Professor exclaimed. "Wincy was right, then, when she said that my companionship would cure him—knowing little minx, isn't she?"

"I shouldn't say it was that altogether," Mrs. Turner objected, "though Angus does seem very chummy with you now. I think he also feels that I love him. To be sure, I always loved him. . . ."

"Most assuredly, my dear."

There was a long pause.

"Perhaps I do love him more deeply since I have the care of him," Mrs. Turner said in a strained voice. "If only I had known when Mark was small—"

Wincy put on her Newfields hat.

"Indirectly," she heard her mother say, "Mrs. Hilliard taught me rather a lot about my three children. Odd, isn't it, that the threat of invasion—"

Her father was singing when Wincy shut the door.

> "God moves in a mysterious way
> His wonders to perform—"

Wincy smiled—as usual, he was quite off key.

I wonder, she said to herself, as she hurried down Banbury Road with her violin-case banging against her leg, whether God will move about Francis the way he did with Mark or whether I'll have to do what I can. But what, she wondered dismally, could I do?

September

XXIII

Wincy had been on the River with Francis.

It was a golden September afternoon and they had punted downstream through the gardens of Iffley Lock toward Sandford.

Wincy had hardly seen him in two months. Then she had run into him in St. Giles one noon. Wearing his best suit and a little white bow-tie, Francis was coming home from the Examination Schools, where he had written the Latin paper. He was jubilant to be done with it.

"Let's celebrate," Wincy had said.

"Do you mean you'd like to?" Francis asked, surprised. "We could go on the River—I didn't think you—"

"Of course I'd like to," Wincy said. "I promised you I'd come some day. I'd been rather expecting—"

Francis looked pleased, and yet worried. The conflicting emotions showed in the curve of his mouth. "Well, I didn't know," he said. "They seem to do things so differently over there—I wasn't sure how you felt."

"Weren't you, Francis?" Wincy asked, giving him a long, reassuring look. If only she could get across to him how much she cared. . . .

The worry disappeared and his mouth settled in a smile.

"We'll go to Sandford," he said happily, and his eyes

206

showed that he was already on the River, seeing Wincy in the punt.

Wincy thought of the don and his wife punting along that day she and Francis had stood on Folly Bridge. The wife had had a tea-basket at her feet and her arms were full of flowers. She had looked sweet, like Aunt Polly.

And now, she, Wincy, would sit in a punt like that and Francis would stand behind her, poling downstream. . . .

But Wincy puzzled over Francis's strange behaviour all the way home. It was so different from the way an American boy would act. Francis seemed to like her, and yet he didn't believe that she liked him. An American boy would have come right out and said so. He would have demanded like a caveman that she make her feelings clear.

Wincy didn't know what to think. Maybe he didn't really like her, maybe he was only being polite. English people are so polite—

At least, they were going to go on the River. They would have a chance to hash things out. They would—if her mother let her go. Wincy wondered how she was going to manage it. Fortunately, Mrs. Turner was at home. Wincy ran right in and asked permission.

Mrs. Turner considered a minute, looking thoughtfully at Wincy. "Why, yes," she said at last, "I think it would be jolly. It's such a ripping day."

"Oh, Mummie, thanks!" Wincy exclaimed. She could hardly believe what she had heard. It had seemed almost hopeless, and then it had been so easy—

"After all," Mrs. Turner said, "you're growing old enough to go punting with a boy we all know. You'll be sixteen soon, Wincy—think of it!"

"Oh—" Wincy said in surprise. Very old, sixteen . . .

"Why don't you take the tea-basket?" Mrs. Turner suggested.

"I didn't know we had one," Wincy said. A *tea-basket*—her joy was complete.

"Of course we have, darling," her mother said. "Daddy and I always used to take it out with us when he was a tutor—before we were married—"

"You and Daddy used to go punting?" Wincy was surprised.

"Naturally. You'll find it in the scullery cupboard. Pack a nice tea for two," Mrs. Turner urged.

It had been super on the River. Francis was in gay spirits at the start, because he was through with Latin forever.

"Did you—" Wincy began and stopped. She didn't like to ask whether he had passed.

Francis understood, though. It was uncanny—he sometimes seemed to read her thoughts.

"I don't know," he said. "I hope so, for Father's sake. It makes no difference to me. You see," he added shyly, looking off beyond the meadows on the bank, "I've—well, I'm not going up to St. James's—I'm joining the Navy."

Wincy was startled. She had been anxious to have Francis do what he most wished. But it had never occurred to her before that if he did join the Navy he would leave Oxford.

"When I come back," he said, not looking at her in his shyness, "I'm going to study engineering. I've decided that, too. It isn't what Father had in mind, but it's what England needs —the England of Tomorrow," he added softly.

"The England of Tomorrow?" Wincy repeated, puzzled.

"Yes," Francis went on, sitting down and letting the punt

drift, "there'll be so much to do—rebuilding the bombed areas
—London and Bristol and Coventry. You must have noticed
the frightful mess as you came through London."

"Some," Wincy said. "A few houses—" She didn't remember much.

"But, Wincy, there are acres and acres of demolished areas.
How could you help seeing them?"

"We weren't in London very long," Wincy explained. "Just
going across in a taxi from St. Pancras to Paddington with
that lady who looked out for us on the boat. And I was so
homesick for Belmont, I guess I just didn't notice."

This seemed to puzzle Francis. He was quiet for a bit.
Wincy watched him looking down into the shallow water.
There were weeds on the bottom, grey-green, quite un-
troubled by the current of the River.

"There'll be a need for engineers and architects—so much
to do," he went on finally. "But we mustn't leave it to stuffy
people, else they'll rebuild England to look like the Albert
Memorial."

"Architecture," Wincy repeated thoughtfully, "I'd never
thought of doing that. It would be fun building houses. I'd
like that—houses, not all in a row, hiding behind a wall, like in
Banbury Road, but set down here and there, any old way,
with gardens all around, instead of just at the back."

"It isn't the bombed areas alone," Francis said, "but all those
frightful slums in London. We want to clear them away, put
in a central heating plant for the whole neighbourhood—"

"I'd never thought of becoming an architect," Wincy put
in in a determined voice, "but I think that would suit me very
well. I'm glad you're going to do the things you really wish,

Francis—the Navy and the England of Tomorrow—" She opened the basket and gave him his tea.

"So am I," he said, biting into a bun, and added shyly, "if it hadn't been for you, Wincy, I never would have done. It's the way you've gone ahead with things you thought were right, and what you said about the older generation—"

"What did I say?" Wincy asked, puckering her forehead.

"About it being our world. It is, naturally, but I'd never thought of it before—dim of me."

Wincy looked at his mouth. It was quite firm, yet even now there was a good-natured curve to the corners.

"Yes," she said, looking at him, "it's our world."

Francis's Adam's apple had begun bobbing up and down. He pulled one of the crinkly rushes from the River and played with it.

"Oh," he exclaimed, smiling suddenly, "our world—how ripping—I thought you meant our generation's."

"Well, it's both in a way, don't you think?" Wincy asked. "I mean, there's the England of Tomorrow, which we are going to build, and there's our—"

"We could build it together," Francis said happily, "you and I. We could make a sort of combine—you designing the houses and I putting in the appliances and doing the engineering for a whole area. It would be jolly, only—" Joy and enthusiasm suddenly seemed extinguished in him.

Wincy could not understand such a rapid change in mood. He had almost put into words her own feeling. It had almost been a very important moment again, a moment which would determine the course of their whole lives. And then Francis's feeling had collapsed, like a pricked balloon.

Didn't he like her? He had seemed to, for a moment, until he suddenly had a thought which changed everything. What could it be?

Francis was fiddling with the lid of the tea-basket. It was a very old basket and the straw that bound the lid to it had worn thin. If he fiddled with it much longer, it would break. But Wincy couldn't very well ask him to stop.

"Wincy," he said suddenly, obviously struggling to say the thing that had made his happiness collapse, "are the Hilliards Mormons?"

Now what in the world did that have to do with his feeling for her? Was he trying to change the subject?

"No," Wincy said impatiently, "of course not. Aunt Polly's a Unitarian and Uncle Bill—I don't think he's anything."

"Oh," Francis said, puzzled. "I thought perhaps it was because they were Mormons that you—"

"Mormons live out West somewhere."

"Oh well," Francis sighed, "then that's not it. I just thought perhaps—"

"What?"

"Well, Mormons have a lot of wives, don't they?"

"I don't know. What of it?"

"I thought perhaps you had been influenced by that," Francis explained seriously. "I mean—well, you rather seem to like me, and yet you were so matey with that American chap who came to visit you."

"Hank," Wincy put in. He ought to know the name by now and stop saying "that chap."

Hank's name echoed in Wincy's head. Maybe it was the River that carried the sound, though it seemed to be inside her. It seemed as though she had shouted the name in one of those caverns which echo and re-echo, sending it back to her from a distance.

"Mother told me about it," Francis said.

About what? Wincy wondered. She couldn't imagine what he was talking about.

"Oh," she exclaimed suddenly, seeing Picklepuss all crumpled on the window-seat, charmed by Wincy's music, "*that*." Picklepuss had said those nasty things because she had seen Wincy throw her arms about Hank when he arrived.

Wincy ought not to have behaved that way. Her mother had been right—she saw it now. It made Francis think she was boy-crazy. But she had been young then—now she was almost sixteen, seeing things so differently . . .

Francis turned the punt about and began poling. It seemed no time at all before they reached the landing-stage at Folly Bridge and he helped her out.

"D'you know," he said, "it's two months since the day I met you here."

So Francis was counting time from that important moment, too . . . Wincy's heart, which had been down, suddenly soared.

They parted at St. Giles Church. Francis looked melancholy. His Adam's apple was bouncing and he was twiddling the grip on his handlebar.

I ought to tell him not to do that, Wincy thought. He'll wear it loose. But she said nothing.

Then suddenly, she giggled. It wasn't because Francis looked so melancholy and his Adam's apple was behaving so badly, but he might have thought so, for he looked offended and suddenly biked home.

Wincy was sorry. She hadn't meant to hurt his feelings.

She had merely understood, all at once, what Francis had been driving at when he asked if the Hilliards were Mormons. That was what made her giggle. He thought she loved two boys at the same time—one American and one English. People had such funny notions about America. She hadn't understood when he asked her, or she might have explained. She would have told Francis that Hank—that Hank had—well—gone out of her life.

If only I had understood then—how dim of me, she thought. Now he thinks I'm making fun of him.

Wincy went home slowly. It was strange—she had been so happy on the River, yet now that she was coming home, she was sad. How could one's feelings change so quickly? That was the way Francis was acting—first soaring, and then down in the dumps. She had never been that way before. Was she sick—ill?

Or maybe—could it be—love?

XXIV

"I met Beveridge coming out of University this morning," Professor Turner said. "We stopped to talk. Very ingenious, some of his ideas—"

"Oh yes," Mrs. Turner murmured absently, squinting at the needle she was threading.

"Quite a difference of opinion, though, about the merits of his plan," the Professor remarked. "What do you think, Wincy?"

Wincy's forehead puckered. She didn't know anything

about the plan. The Hilliards had been quite excited, she remembered, when it was first announced, but she had never heard it mentioned in Oxford. No, she didn't know anything about it.

"What do you think?" her father asked again.

Mischief bubbled up in Wincy. "Little girls don't hold political opinions," she said.

But Professor Turner did not recognize the words which he had spoken the day after Wincy returned from America, when she gave Doctor Quelch her opinion about India. "Come," he urged, "you're not a little girl any more. You're almost sixteen."

Yes, she felt old. Francis hadn't been to see her since the day, a fortnight ago, when they had been on the River. She wanted to explain why she had giggled when she suddenly understood what he was driving at, asking about Mormons. She wanted to see him, just to see him. But he hadn't come.

Now, she said to herself, I understand why they call childhood the golden age. . . . In Belmont this strange thing hadn't had the power to touch her. She had been too young. Sandy Whipple had been nuts about her, the girls said. Maybe he had felt this way and she hadn't understood. But she did now. She felt sorry for Sandy. He had been such a friendly kid. His freckles and his funny ginger hair. . . .

Mrs. Turner was smiling at Wincy. "John," she asked playfully, "have you ever noticed anything odd about Francis Quelch's mouth?"

"Francis Quelch's mouth?" the Professor repeated. "Never even noticed that the boy had a mouth, though I suppose he must have, or I should have done."

"Haven't you ever noticed," Mrs. Turner went on, "the

way it's not made up its mind yet whether to be good natured or firm? Wincy thinks it's going to be firm in the middle but jolly at the corners."

"Sounds ridiculous," Professor Turner said. "But Francis got full marks in his Latin paper. I saw it this afternoon."

Wincy's heart jumped.

"How nice," Mrs. Turner said. "Quelch will be pleased."

"It was amazingly good," the Professor continued. "I had feared it would be merely fair to middling. Astonishing how easy it was to teach that lad, once I understood the workings of his mind."

Wincy was happy Francis had done well, but why hadn't he come to tell her? He knew she was anxious about the results: he had practically read her mind that day on the River. Besides, she wanted to explain to him about Hank—that he was nothing more than just a foster-cousin. But Francis never came.

Now that he had passed his exams, he would be able to do all the things he dreamed of when he came back from the war, building up the England of Tomorrow. While he was away, Wincy must not be wasting her time.

"Daddy," she asked, and she suddenly felt shy, "do you think I could go to Somerville?"

"Somerville?" Professor Turner repeated incredulously.

"Yes. Do you think I could? Miss Fulleylove says I'm doing rather well this term."

"Somerville?" Professor Turner repeated. First surprise and then tremendous joy came into his face. "My dear, how perfectly splendid that you should want to go up! I had hoped that you would follow in my footsteps—not necessarily classics, but some branch of higher learning—"

"Architecture," Wincy broke in, unable to keep it to her-self any longer. "You know, after the war. . . ." She saw it all again the way Francis had described it—the bombed areas that would need rebuilding, the modern little houses going up where the frightful slums had been. She had only just dis-covered the need for all this and she presumed that her parents had not known of it, either. Her enthusiasm increased as she told about it.

Professor Turner listened with such interest that Wincy was certain he was hearing about these things for the first time.

"Yes indeed," he said. "You are right—there will be great work to be done. England must be rebuilt in many ways, not alone her houses. She must be healed of the wounds of war."

"Funny thing," Wincy said thoughtfully, "I hadn't noticed these things about England before. I mean, just because no bombs fell around here I didn't think—"

"I'd been wondering," the Professor broke in, "how long it would take until you discovered your own country. That's why I was so surprised just now, when you spoke of these things. It's the first time."

"Oh," Wincy said. Her father was right. "I wonder why."

What has happened to me? she asked herself. . . . Even as Francis had looked quite different to her that day on Folly Bridge, so the world about her looked new. She saw its de-tails for the first time, as she had noticed little things about Francis which set him apart from all the other boys around Oxford.

"You were too wrapped up in your adjustment to your mother and myself, I presume," the Professor was saying, "and too nostalgic for America—which was only natural. But

I'm ever so glad you've awakened to the needs of England—
the England of Tomorrow, as you call it."

"I didn't think of it myself," Wincy admitted honestly. "It
was Francis."

Mrs. Turner looked at Wincy and smiled like a conspirator.
They shared a secret.

"I guess I was rather self-centered," Wincy said in a low
voice. She looked out of the window. Francis . . . if only he
were there—

It was the Professor's turn to look mischievous. "You'll have
to do construe, you know, for Somerville," he said gloatingly.

Wincy looked up quickly. "But Latin doesn't have anything to do with architecture—the architecture in the England
of Tomorrow," she protested. "We don't want to be stuffy,"
Wincy added sternly, "and rebuild England so it looks like the
Albert Memorial."

"My dear," Professor Turner began, "the classics, as I con-
ceived them before you opened my eyes to other things—
these, perhaps, have only a remote connection with the future."

"That's what I mean—"

"But," the Professor continued, "the England of Tomorrow—on what foundation will your generation build it? On
the England of the Present. And on what foundation was
this England built?"

"Why, the past," Wincy answered. "Of course—how dim
of me. Oh, well—" Francis had managed the Latin, in spite
of all his worrying. She would like doing things he had done.
"I'll take it," she said.

She would go to Somerville like Daphne Godstow and have
lots of friends and do tons of jolly things.

"Latin can be very stimulating, actually," her father was saying, "since I have a new undergraduate approach—"

"Daddy," Wincy broke in, "what *is* the Undergraduate Approach, anyway?" She had often tried to find out and had always been put off.

Professor Turner laughed. "That's merely a sort of telegraphic code expression we use at St. James's," he explained.

"But what does it stand for? It's bothered you a lot."

"Yes, it did, though I hadn't realized you knew. Some Fellows feel that we ought to approach the undergraduates quite differently, offering them more significant weapons for the life they are about to take up—not technical training, you understand, but a new approach to the old classical studies."

"Sounds all right," Wincy said.

"Yes, it is. I felt so from the first," her father agreed. "Nevertheless, I was bound by habit to certain methods of teaching. But Quelch can't see the need for any change whatever. When he becomes Warden, I fear there will be even greater difficulties, for I have become extremely radical in my views."

"*Radical*, Daddy?"

"Well, for St. James's . . ." the Professor replied, smiling. "Last spring I was troubled because I could not make the classics more meaningful to my students. The Undergraduate Approach was like the riddle of the sphinx. It was your introducing me to psychology that gave me the key. Like Oedipus, I have solved the riddle."

"Oedipus?" Wincy repeated. "You mean Freud?"

"No, my dear, I do not. I mean Sophocles. I trust that things have not yet come to such a pass that Freud has immortalized Sophocles," he said, laughing.

"Psychology," Wincy murmured. Perhaps psychology would help her with Francis.

It was a fortnight since they had been on the River, yet he hadn't come once. He no longer needed Latin texts explained, so he had no reason for stopping in to see Professor Turner. And he didn't seem to care to come simply to see Wincy. She never ran into him in St. Giles, although she often cruised about there on her bicycle, in case he should happen along.

When she was little and didn't care for him, Francis was always about, pulling her plaits, having tea in the nursery, and being somewhat of a nuisance generally. But now, when she wanted him so badly that she thought she'd pop, he never turned up. Life was a mess. . . .

Wincy tried to figure out a way to make Francis understand how she really felt. Psychology had worked well with Angus and her parents. But you couldn't use psychology on a boy who wasn't even around. Besides, she didn't really see how it would work in the case of love.

Psychology's no use at all when you're in love, Wincy decided. God must move—there's nothing I can do.

October

XXV

"There was some ginger-beer in the College cellars," Professor Turner said. "The Manciple presented it to me when I told him we were having a Hallowe'en party."

"Congratters!" Angus exclaimed.

Mrs. Turner was putting the finishing touches on the jack-o'-lanterns. She had cut some eerie creatures out of gourds and vegetable marrow. They were lined up on the kitchen table and she stood off to admire the effect.

"They're beauties," Angus said, rolling out pie-crust.

"You managed to get such tons of food, Mummie," Wincy exclaimed. "Everything looks so good."

"It *was* rather a job of work queueing up," Mrs. Turner admitted.

Professor Turner was peeling and slicing the apples. "Angus, fetch me the cup we always put in the centre of the tart," he asked, putting down the paring knife and licking his finger. "You know, the one with the broken handle."

"Oh, no, Daddy," Wincy protested, "not in an American pie."

"How else do they keep the crust from falling in?" Mrs. Turner asked.

Wincy and Angus laughed.

"They fill it with apples," Angus explained.

"Clever," Mrs. Turner conceded, "but what a lot of apples."

Her husband began peeling again. He was determined to make this an authentic Hallowe'en party. But every few moments he stopped to lick the blister that had risen on his finger.

Angus looked at the makings of the pie: the dough and the neat slices of apple, the cinnamon that had been so hard to come by. "There really ought to be cheese," he said, "or ice cream for pie all o' mud."

"All of mud?" Mrs. Turner repeated, anxiously.

"Oh," Angus murmured, "skip it—I mean, let it pass."

"How did you ever come to think of giving a Hallowe'en party, Rachel?" Professor Turner asked, looking at his wife in admiration.

Mrs. Turner finished sticking the candle in a jack-o'-lantern before answering. "It was a most peculiar thing," she said, "the way it struck me all of a heap at the fishmongers. I was buying haddock and thinking—" she hesitated. "I was thinking how sweet these children are," she finished shyly.

Wincy and Angus looked up, startled.

"What a strange setting for maternal reveries," the Professor exclaimed, laughing.

"But they are sweet, John. I'm beginning to feel such pride in them. Love I always had toward them, but pride grows with children, I believe."

"Oh, Mummie," Wincy cried, throwing her arms about her mother and hugging her.

Mrs. Turner patted Wincy's arm. "And then, as I was passing the American Red Cross Club on my way home," she continued, "I remembered what Harley had said about Hallowe'en in Africa—how dismal it would be. The children had mentioned at brekker about tonight being Hallowe'en. So I popped in to see the matron, or whatever they call her, a charming young person from South Carolina."

In her earnest desire to explain how her plan had originated, Mrs. Turner stopped working. Wincy finished putting in the candles.

"How do you know which state she comes from?" Professor Turner inquired curiously.

"I asked her."

"My dear," the Professor said, laughing, "you've come all over American, asking personal questions of a total stranger."

"And she said," Mrs. Turner continued, pretending not to notice that her husband was pulling her leg, "I think she said, for I couldn't understand too well, that it would be *swell* if we had a party and she would send round half a dozen lonely boys."

But we don't know any of them, Wincy thought dismally. I don't really want anyone, since Francis isn't coming. . . .

"It will mean a lot to those lads," the Professor said, frilling the edge of the pie.

Mrs. Turner had kept the best news for the last. "One of them," she finished proudly, "comes from Belmont, Massachusetts."

Instantly, Wincy looked up. Could it be Hank? No, if he were in Oxford, he would have let her know. How she wished it might be—Hank was steadfast. He liked Wincy, and he didn't turn cold on her suddenly, the way Francis had done. Hank and she spoke the same language. She didn't have to explain the simplest things, like that business about Mormons, for instance.

Francis, it's true, had seemed to read her thoughts, but that was probably a coincidence, both of them happening to think of the same things at the same time. At any rate, it was all over—why, she didn't know, but she suspected that, although he had liked her to start with, he couldn't get around the feeling he had about her having left England during the blitz. It might not even be resentment. It might be just the fact that owing to her long absence, Wincy was no longer in close touch with the things that had happened in England. That, of course, was why she and Hank spoke the same language. They had grown up together in America.

But it had been childish to think that some day she might marry Hank. He was not only steadfast, he was sweet. And yet, there was a sort of roughness about him: his way of saying things right out, anything he happened to think, and of asking the most personal questions. Besides, she intended visiting the Hilliards after the war, but she couldn't live in America always. That wouldn't be the way to get caught up in England.

Francis, she whispered to herself, Francis . . . why couldn't he have been the steadfast one?

"Jolly good!" Professor Turner was saying to his wife as he pushed the pie into the oven. "Belmont is not a large place. The lad is doubtless acquainted with the Hilliards. Angus, perhaps he can give us news of Joseph."

"Joseph who?"

"What *is* his surname?" the Professor asked himself, pausing to think with a potholder in either hand. "Very odd, as I recall. Don't you remember? When you first came home you were much concerned about his welfare."

But Angus did not remember at all.

"Joseph," Professor Turner repeated, gazing at the ceiling for inspiration. "I know it was Joseph." His face brightened as he turned to Angus. "Yes—Joseph Palooka."

"Oh, him—" Angus said indifferently. After a pause he went on eagerly, "We're reading the jolliest story in construe this term—all about two chaps who were brought up by a wolf and fed by a woodpecker."

"I suspect you refer to Romulus and Remus," his father said.

Angus looked confused. "No, not Uncle Remus," he explained. "Some chaps in Rome—I didn't listen to their names. I was thinking what a posh picture Sabu could make of it," he added dreamily.

English and American people don't really speak the same language, Wincy thought. That's the whole trouble. Because the words happen to be the same, they think they can understand each other, but half the time they mean slightly different things. It would almost be better if they spoke quite different languages. Then people would make allowances for the strangeness.

"I've invited Daphne Godstow," Mrs. Turner was saying, "and Brenda and Francis."

Wincy, carrying mugs into the dining room, almost dropped the lot as she heard her mother's words. He was coming after all—he was coming after all—oh, it would be a beautiful party. Even though he did not care about her, she would see him again—his nice eyes, the fall of his sandy hair, his determined, good-natured mouth. . . .

Oh beautiful, beautiful world, Wincy sang inside her head as she flew back to the kitchen for more mugs, Francis is coming to the party—

"Of course," Mrs. Turner was saying, "Francis cannot come as it's his last night at home."

His last night at home . . . there was a bitter taste in Wincy's mouth. He wasn't even coming to say good-bye to her.

"The name of the new Warden will be announced tonight," Professor Turner said. "The Fellows convene for election this afternoon."

"Then you won't be home for the party?" Angus asked, worried.

"Of course I shall, my boy," his father promised, smiling. "Nothing, not even the election of a new Warden, could keep me from attending our Hallowe'en party. I shall excuse myself when the votes have been cast," he explained to his wife. "It's the merest formality, in any case. We all know what the result will be."

Yes, thought Wincy, we all know what the result will be for the Turners when Picklepuss becomes Mrs. Warden.

"I do so wish Mark might have been here for the party," Mrs. Turner said wistfully. "It would have been ever so jolly. Pity Francis can't come, too. It would have been a nice send-off."

"The result of the election will be a nice send-off for him," the Professor remarked.

"I don't think it will mean very much," Mrs. Turner said. "They're quite certain of it already—Monica said so this morning. Warden Godstow has the deciding vote, and Quelch knows he can count on him."

"Of course."

Disconsolately, Wincy tested the apples which Angus had hung from the rafters to make certain that they were securely tied. He had brought the washing tubs into the kitchen and was filling them with water.

What was the use of all these preparations? Francis wasn't coming. . . .

XXVI

WINCY STOOD looking into the little mirror between the windows. She had been brushing her hair for ever so long, but she was not pleased.

It was ages now since anyone at Newfields had called her the Yankee, but—even in the gym-tunic—she never felt she looked *quite* like the others. She knew, though she hated to admit it, that this was because of her hair. It had grown so long since it was bobbed seven months ago in Sally Sutton's beauty-parlour, that she had had to put the ends up in curl-papers. The long curls made her look foreign: Newfields girls didn't look like that because Veronica Lake hadn't entered their life.

Wincy took one more long look in the mirror, and then, without hesitating another moment, she grasped the scissors and cut her hair. The curls lay in bright patches all about her on the floor.

But Wincy did not look at them. She was looking at her head, turning and twisting to get a better view of the back. It was not very even, but she was satisfied: she had that tidy Newfields look.

Angus came in to have his face blackened. He was so engrossed in his costume that he did not notice Wincy's hair. He was not going to the party as a ghost this year, the way he had always done in Belmont. Draping himself with sheets had no appeal for Angus now. Instead, he had made himself a gorgeous skeleton costume by chalking bones onto the black-out curtain his mother had given him.

"You're a gruesome sight," Wincy said as she blackened his face.

What should she wear for the party—Sally Sutton's dirndl? Since her mother had called the dress outlandish when Wincy unpacked it, she had never worn it in Oxford. For Hallowe'en, though, something like that might be appropriate.

"It's going to be wizard," Angus said happily. "I wish Mark was coming."

And Francis, Wincy thought, but she said nothing.

"I say, Wincy, d'you know," Angus said eagerly, "I'm going to be hooker in scrum tomorrow." He looked at her expectantly through his black make-up.

But Wincy did not answer him. She was thinking of the boys who were coming to the party.

"I don't mean to swank," Angus added in a superior tone, when he did not receive the admiration he craved, "but it's as good as being first base."

"I know that," Wincy answered loftily. "Don't think I don't know all about rugger."

"It's a ripping game," Angus said with such an inward glow that Wincy could see the game had completely won him over.

"Clear off now," she said, giving him a little shove, "you look terrifying."

The door of her mother's room was open and Wincy could hear her talking to Professor Turner, who was in his dressing-room.

"Monica was doubtful about letting Brenda come," she was saying. "She was just beginning one of her homilies about girls that age—"

Girls-your-age, Wincy thought, mimicking Mrs. Quelch's high-pitched voice to herself.

"I gave her no chance," Mrs. Turner continued. "I said, 'Monica, your daughter will not be defiled by contact with those wholesome young Americans. It will do her good, actually. She might even lose some of her inhibitions.'"

"Did you really, Rachel?" Professor Turner asked, and Wincy could hear his hearty laugh.

"I did. But I doubt she knows what inhibitions are. I said, 'If you take my advice, you will send Brenda to America after the war for a bit of study.'"

The Professor seemed to be pondering this, for it was some time before he spoke. "It depends," he said, "what sort of people Brenda would fall in with. The Hilliards made a profound impression on our children and I shudder to think what would have happened if the impression had not been a good one. We were very fortunate that it was the Hilliards who offered them a home."

"That's so," Wincy heard her mother say.

"And although I knew nothing whatsoever about Hilliard," her father continued, "when I heard that he was attached to Harvard, I felt instantly reassured. I knew the children would not be changed fundamentally—" he dropped his voice a little but Wincy could still hear him, "morals and so on." Then he added, "D'you know, Rachel, university people are much the same the world over."

There was a silence.

Presently Mrs. Turner said thoughtfully, "It had never occurred to me that the Hilliards might be people like us—not in the least."

What a mad thought! It made Wincy laugh—her parents like the Hilliards. . . . The Hilliards were sweet, but nobody could be quite so nice as her parents.

How lucky she had been, though, to go to Belmont. If she had stopped at home, she would still be half tied to the nursery. And her lovely American friends—she would never have made them. If the soldiers who were coming to the party were like Hank and the Agassiz boys, she would like them. But would Daphne? Wincy did hope so. She probably would, for most American boys were nice.

Wincy had taken out the dirndl and spread it on her bed. Instantly it brought back Sally Sutton—Sally wearing it to parties, to school dances. There was one time at Agassiz . . . Wincy couldn't remember, but it must have been Christmas, or perhaps graduation—now wasn't it strange that events in Belmont should seem blurred already? It was hardly more than half a year since she had left.

Yet, she remembered, events had already begun to recede in her very last hour there, when she and Angus and the Hilliards had driven through Cambridge on the way to the Boston dock.

The taxi-driver's radio was playing boogie-woogie. Through the closed window, as they drove past, Wincy could see people talking—two of the boys from Hank's house standing in front of the "Coop," and Dean Dunlap greeting the cop who directed the traffic in Harvard Square—but she couldn't hear their voices. Seeing their lips form words yet hearing only music gave the impression of a movie. Though Wincy was still in Cambridge, it was as if she had already left and was seeing it in a movie—true in each detail, but nevertheless unreal.

Now even the details were blurred. Wincy didn't mind, really. There were happier memories to take the place of the others—all the jolly times she had spent with Daphne and that lovely afternoon on the River with Francis. She would never forget that, even the smallest details of their punt and their tea and the things that Francis had said.

Wincy opened the silver buttons of the dirndl and held up the shirred blouse to examine it.

Mrs. Turner, crossing the landing on her way to the bathroom, peeped in.

"Shall you wear that?" she asked approvingly. "It's really lovely. I can't think why you never wore it before." She stopped suddenly, aghast. "*Wincy*, what *have* you done to your hair?"

Wincy turned around so that her mother could get a good view of the back. "Do you like it, Mummie? I think it's no end more English, don't you?"

"Well, I don't know," Mrs. Turner said sadly. "Yes, it is more English, but I rather liked the way you wore your hair before. It suited you. There was something attractively—" she searched for the right word, "individual about it—quite individual." She left the room, looking greatly disappointed.

But Wincy wasn't disappointed. She gave only a casual glance to the circle of yellow curls lying on the floor. They belonged to her past. She was looking toward the England of Tomorrow.

She would build it, and Francis would build it, she thought sorrowfully, but not together, as they had planned that day on the River. "We could make a sort of combine," he had said.

But that was all over. How could she look forward to the England of Tomorrow with a boy who didn't even come to see her in the England of Today? That thing Daddy had said about building the future on the foundations of the past and present. . . . It was certainly true.

Wincy considered the dirndl a long time. It was lovely, but somehow she couldn't see herself wearing it in Oxford. It would look queer. She hung it on the hanger again and put it in the wardrobe.

When the doorbell clanged, she was tying the sash of the frock her mother had had made over for her to wear to the Warden's garden party.

XXVII

LOOKING VERY festive in one of the orange hats Angus had made for the party, Professor Turner came out to the larder to fetch the pie. Wincy was in the scullery washing the forks so that they could be used over again, just as the Hilliards did when they gave a party.

There was a tremendous racket in the dining room. The American soldiers had not been in the house five minutes before they began talking to the Turners and Daphne and Brenda as if they had known them all their lives. Not one had mentioned the weather.

"The pie looks lovely, Daddy," Wincy said appreciatively as her father passed her with it in his hand.

The Professor stopped to tip up Wincy's chin and peer into her face. "Happy with your Americans, chicken?"

"No."

"But, Wincy," Professor Turner exclaimed, "you used to be so keen about Americans. And these lads are ever so amusing, only I'm disappointed in the one from Belmont: he doesn't know the Hilliards."

"They're all right," Wincy admitted, pouring the coffee, "but crude, don't you think? I'd give the lot of them for one English chap."

Her father smiled knowingly. "He'll come back, my dear," he said.

Wincy gave her father a wan smile. He was nice. But he didn't know about her trouble with Francis. If they could only have hashed everything out, she and Francis, they might have parted good friends. . . .

She placed the coffee cups on the tray, not bothering to try and match the saucers. The dishes were even more nicked than when she and Angus came home, but Wincy didn't mind. She almost felt a pride in their brokenness. They were part of the England of Today. Delicate Spode belonged to the past and maybe to the future, but certainly not to this party.

Going back into the dining room, Wincy blinked. It was dark, except for the eerie shadows of the jack-o'-lanterns flickering on the chocolate-coloured walls.

"Jeepers!" the boy called Butch exclaimed as Wincy came in with the tray. "Coffee with the grub, just like home—None of this Buckingham Palace after-dinner stuff. Nice going—"

"Unh, unh," the one they called Tex drawled, shaking his head. "It's okay by me having it after supper. When I get back to my home town, I'm going to start a new style. It's mighty nice."

Mrs. Turner was talking to the man they called Horny.

"We were all playing a charming symphony," Wincy heard her say, "when we looked round and there he stood."

Her mother, Wincy thought, smiling to herself, *her mother* describing the most intimate family scene to a stranger!

The boy from Belmont proposed a toast to the Turners. He stood holding his ginger-beer in the air. But the other boys went right on talking.

Tex seemed to have gone quite potty over Daphne. He was talking without let-up, telling her in his deep, southern voice about his home. "Miles and miles of cotton," he was saying, stretching out his arms, "as far as the eye can see—not a hedge or a tree."

Wincy was embarrassed. She kept watching Daphne to see whether she was revolted by all this chatter, but Daphne seemed fascinated.

The other two soldiers were taking a wicked delight in making Brenda giggle. She was struggling to be sedate, but at one moment it almost looked as though she would have to leave the table—she was laughing so hard with her mouth full of ginger-beer.

Like a dragonfly, Angus darted about in his skeleton costume. He had borrowed Baby Palmer's rattle again and was shaking it under the black-out curtain to give a greater illusion of reality to his painted bones.

Mrs. Turner had held back one surprise and now she went to the dresser and brought it out.

"Oh," Daphne exclaimed with delight, "crackers!"

"D'you mean biscuits?" Angus asked, running over to see. "I didn't think you could get them."

"Snappers," the boy from Belmont explained, holding out his hand to Angus. "Here—pull!"

His name was Vin O'Reilly and he was nice looking. His G.I. haircut and the way he talked reminded Wincy of Hank, but of course he wasn't so nice as that. He had fallen hard for Wincy the moment he arrived and he didn't care who knew it.

When Wincy passed him his coffee, he jumped up and placed a chair for her next to his. "Come and sit side of me," he begged, without a trace of shyness. Only an American boy would smile at a girl like that the very first time they met.

Yes, he was a lot like Hank. It made her feel as though she had known him for years, instead of only an hour. It really was true: she clicked with American boys.

"Golly," Vin was saying, looking at Wincy as if she were something good to eat, "it's swell seeing an American girl."

"I'm not American," Wincy blurted out crossly. "I should think you could tell the difference."

"Well, you've lived in Belmont," Vin argued, still staring at her without even trying to hide his feeling. "Your father told me about it."

From the head of the table, Professor Turner glanced up, beaming.

Vin looked so familiar that it seemed strange Wincy had never met him in Belmont. Perhaps she used to pass his house. She thought of all the streets and wondered where it stood.

"Whereabouts did you live?" he was asking.

"That's just what I was wondering about you," Wincy said. Could he read her thoughts, too, like Francis? "You know Concord Avenue?" she asked. "Well, you go out under the railroad bridge till you come to the hill where, if you look back, you can see Boston—the dome of the State House—"

Suddenly, as she spoke, it rushed over her like the wiry,

warm water in the Hilliards' shower—all the happiness and excitement and intimacies of those years. She saw the hill again as it looked when she was biking down to Agassiz, or the way it dropped away terrifyingly as she and a bunch of kids went sliding down on skis. She saw the Hilliards' house with the trumpet-vine growing across the fanlight, Uncle Bill and Aunt Polly sitting in the glider on the porch and Sutty coiled in the hose as he sprinkled the lawn. She saw it all, but not achingly, the way she had before. It was pure joy.

Vin was explaining where he lived, but Wincy didn't hear a word. She tried to pull herself back, to look interested, but she could only think of the Belmont which Vin didn't know.

She wouldn't have missed those years for anything. People were wrong if they thought being away had made her any less English. Sometimes looking at a place from the distance gave you a better view of it. People seemed to forget that. Francis had. She might have been able to make him see it, though, if he had only come around. Too bad she didn't have the same appeal for him she had for Hank and Vin. . . .

The bell clanged. Had Francis come after all? Wincy flew to the door.

It was Warden Godstow.

"I'm bringing a bit of news, Winifred," he whispered, hanging his greatcoat on one of the branching arms.

Wincy turned to him eagerly.

"At the meeting this evening," he began solemnly in the tone of a conspirator, but suddenly, hearing the noise in the drawing room, he stopped and looked around.

"It's the Hallowe'en party," Wincy explained. "Daphne is here."

The Warden nodded. "What about—" he hesitated. "Is

Madame Picklepuss here, too?" he asked finally, looking like a wicked little boy.

Wincy burst out laughing. "No," she answered gaily, "she's not."

The Warden looked relieved. "At the meeting this evening," he repeated, taking Wincy's hands and looking down at her fondly, "your father was elected Warden of St. James's."

"My father—you mean Daddy? The new Warden? But Doctor Quelch—"

"Your father, Winifred," the Warden repeated solemnly. "We need a man with modern views who is sensitive to young minds," the Warden went on, "who can turn his hand to anything; who can concoct a dumpling, if need be, as well as a dissertation—" he laughed, but continued seriously, "a man interested in music and science as well as the humanities. You will readily see, Winifred," he said, squeezing Wincy's hand happily, "that your father is eminently fitted to be entrusted with this post."

"Oh, Warden Godstow," she gasped, "how swell—" The American expression slipped out to her own surprise. "How wizard, I mean," she exclaimed.

The Warden hadn't noticed the slip, for the racket in the dining room had become terrific. One of the boys was playing "Home on the Range" on a mouth-organ. Very soon they were all singing.

"Play: 'Casey Jones,'" Wincy heard someone shout. They all joined in with their barber-shop harmony and Wincy thought the roof would pop off.

But the Warden was fascinated. "Delightful," he shouted, in order to make himself heard. "Isn't it delightful?"

Wincy didn't think so. "Rather crude," she said.

"But, Winifred—" the old gentleman exclaimed, disappointed, "I thought you liked American music."

"I do," she answered, as the singers swung to "Chattanooga Choo-choo." "But madrigals are ever so much nicer."

The Warden laughed.

"Well, I see you are becoming a little insular," he said. "Young people often are. But never fear, Winifred. You will appreciate these things, too, when you are my age."

The old gentleman turned toward the dining room. His childish face was radiant.

"Come and meet the American soldiers," Wincy begged.

"Yes," he said, and added in a whisper, "I've brought my flute." He tapped the pocket of his greatcoat. "Perhaps later, when they've done with their festivities—the *Toy Symphony*!"

At the door of the dining room, the Warden stopped, blinking. The weird jack-o'-lanterns glowed in the darkness. Into the jagged mouth of one of them, Professor Turner had inserted his pipe.

Barely visible in the darkness, Professor and Mrs. Turner came forward in welcome.

"How nice!" Mrs. Turner exclaimed, joy vibrating in her voice.

When her eyes became accustomed to the darkness, Wincy saw that Professor Turner had a book in his hand. Even at a party, she thought . . . But she was surprised when he opened it and, holding up a candle, turned to the Warden.

"I've been showing our American guests the present Wincy brought me from the States," he explained. "Do see this witty concept of the Olympians."

"Ah, yes," the Warden said, "I remember the film. It was superb!"

"I've come in, Turner, to tell you," the Warden began, taking the Professor's hand, "that at the meeting this evening—"

Wincy did not hear the rest of Warden Godstow's announcement. The doorbell had clanged again.

Francis was at the door, Francis was in the passage. He had come—beautiful, beautiful world. . . .

He would not join the party, as there was no time, he said. He had only come for a moment. He stood looking down at Wincy with a troubled expression, as if he were lost in the woods and did not know which way to go.

"Have you heard—" she asked, "about the Warden?"

"Yes," Francis said. "As soon as Father came home, I knew by his face that he hadn't—"

"I'm sorry about Doctor Quelch," Wincy broke in. "Was he terribly disappointed?"

"No, I don't think he cares. He wasn't so keen for it, really," Francis said thoughtfully. "It was Mother."

Wincy nodded. Poor Mrs. Quelch must feel frightfully after pulling all those wires to get her husband elected.

"I'm glad for your sake, Wincy," Francis said sportingly, "that it's your father. That's what I came to say."

"Oh," Wincy exclaimed. It was nice of him, but was that all he had come to say? "Francis, remember what you said, a long time ago, about St. James's being the same as in the Middle Ages? Well, you just wait and see what it's going to be like now. We're going to make things hum."

Francis laughed. He looked so nice when he laughed, the

corners of his mouth curling and his eyes so bright and happy. . . .

Mrs. Turner's voice brought Wincy's thoughts back. "And now," she was announcing, "we are going to repair to the scullery. We are informed that that is the proper place for the damper aspects of a Hallowe'en party."

The boys cheered. "Attaboy!" one of them shouted.

Francis smiled. "Sounds jolly," he said.

"Tell me," Wincy begged shyly, "was it because I was evacuated that you—you—" She didn't know how to put it.

But Francis understood. He was reading her thoughts again, only they were hard to answer. He stared at the floor of the passage.

"I didn't think there was much use," he said slowly, twisting the ends of his necktie. "I mean, you were so frightfully keen about America and all those people—"

He'll wear out his scarf, Wincy thought.

"I bags the first duck," Angus was shouting from the kitchen.

Francis looked surprised. "D'you mean you have ducks?" he asked.

"Ducking for apples," Wincy explained, laughing. "That's what we used to do in Belmont on Hallowe'en. Francis, guess what—I'm going to Somerville."

He looked surprised. "But I thought you wanted to go to that college where your foster-cousin is."

"Oh—Radcliffe. No, I don't want to go there."

"But you said—"

"I did once," Wincy admitted in an off-hand tone, as if it were something she had vaguely considered ages and ages ago, "but I think Somerville will be heaps better for the England of Tomorrow."

"You mean," Francis said—and his face was like the sun suddenly coming out from behind a cloud—"you mean you're going to stop in England after the war?"

"Naturally," Wincy answered impatiently. Why was he so dim?

"Wincy—" he exclaimed, taking the ends of her sash in his hands and crushing them happily.

"I'd love to go to America for a visit," Wincy admitted.

"Oh," Francis put in quickly, "I'd like *that*, too."

Wincy's heart soared. "I'll show it all to you," she said happily. "Belmont and Scituate, and we'll go skiing in Vermont. It'll be jolly. But of course I want to *live* in England."

"Oh, Wincy—" he said, and his Adam's apple began to work, "how dim of me— I was afraid we couldn't join on those jobs—" he looked at her earnestly— "I mean, I couldn't live in a strange country, but if you'll stay in England—"

"Silly," Wincy said softly—sometimes Francis was just a little boy like Angus—"that was what I intended doing all along."

"How dim of me," he repeated, twisting and knotting the ends of Wincy's sash in his emotion.

"Do stop fiddling with my sash, Francis," Wincy said. "You're making a mess of it."

"Oh," he exclaimed, instantly dropping the sash. "Sorry." He took her hand instead and looked at her intently.

"Francis," Wincy asked suddenly, "do you know how long it is since that day we met on Folly Bridge?"

"Three months," he answered instantly.

He did not have to stop and reckon. He counted time from that day, too. . . .

"You know," Wincy said, happily, "it's been like tuning up for a duet—we started with a different pitch—one sharp, the other flat—and then we came closer and closer, till we were in tune."

Very reluctantly, Francis turned to go.

"Cheerio," he said hoarsely, opening the door. But he looked back. "Wincy," he whispered, trying to control his Adam's apple, "do you remember, in the War Memorial Garden at Christ Church—you know, on the ground—'My sword I give to him—'"

"I remember," Wincy said solemnly.

"'My sword I give to him that shall succeed me in my pilgrimage,'" Francis said, grasping Wincy's hand. "I'm giving it to you, Wincy."

And he was gone.

Wincy could not bear to go back to the party. She flopped on the monk's bench, repeating the words to herself, over and over, like a charm.

My sword I give to him—I'm giving it to you. . . .

That puzzled look, as if he had lost his way—that would never be in Francis's face again. And she would never wish for him in that same sharp, hopeless way. Perhaps it would be a long time before he came back, but at least, she would know that if he could, he would come.

"Has everyone had a turn at ducking?" Mrs. Turner asked. "Where's Wincy?"

"I'll find her," Warden Godstow offered, and he came out into the passage, looking very comical in one of Angus's orange hats. "A bit of America transplanted to Banbury Road—what?" he exclaimed, laughing.

Wincy considered. "I don't think it can be done, really—do you, Warden? I mean, it's sort of silly to try."

"I should say you'd been quite successful," the old gentleman said. "Not since the invasion of Poland have I seen such happy faces—not since Munich—"

"I don't mean the party," Wincy explained. "That's Mummie and Daddy's—just—trying to do things here the way we did in Belmont—it's rather idiotic, when you come to think of it. Instead of looking about at England, when we first came home, Angus and I wanted to make everything over—"

"*A l'Americaine*," the Warden put in.

Wincy smiled. She thought how, when she first came home and Doctor Quelch had recited "Oh, to be in England now that April's there," she could only picture Mr. Thurman at Agassiz. How changed she was—

"And whoever wakes in England sees—" she said to herself, thinking of the rest of the poem. She was waking and seeing very fast. . . .

"Come and have your turn in the washing-tub," the Warden urged. "Your mother is looking for you."

He drew Wincy into the bright kitchen and led her to the tub. There were puddles everywhere, but Mrs. Turner did not seem to mind. She was handing out towels lavishly, her precious towels which were wearing so thin, and which could not be replaced without coupons.

If only Francis could have stayed for the party . . . he would have liked these stunts. Some day the war would be over; Francis and Mark would come home. They would have tons of parties like this. . . .

The war would be over! But life wouldn't be a round of fun and parties, Wincy told herself. Houses would have to be planned and built, beautiful new workingmen's homes with gardens all around, set unevenly here and there along the streets of London. Wincy would have to swot so that she would know how to plan and build them.

It would take a great deal of work to set England to rights again, she thought, as she looked at the apples bobbing about in the tub. There were little bites out of some of them, watery white circles with scalloped edges—

Eagerness to get to work at once crowded everything else from Wincy's thought. Even Francis did not seem quite so important. Oh, of course, he was important, very important, but planning for the England of Tomorrow was a very big thing. It was going to take practically all her attention.

She felt powerful, suddenly—strong enough, almost, to put up those houses with her hands—underpinning, sidewalls, rooftrees—she could see them rising from the rubble. . . .

She knew she was capable of doing things, even such great ones as putting England to rights. After all, it hadn't been easy to put things right in Banbury Road, but she had managed that. They were right now.

Very right, oh *very*, Wincy thought, watching her mother mop Horny's dripping head while he, sprawled in Cook's chair, munched the apple he had retrieved from the tub. The Professor stood in the centre of the kitchen, his hands clasped behind his back, trying without success to bite into an apple that dangled from the ceiling. The apple kept slithering out of reach, bobbing away and then bouncing back at him with a smack.

Not such an easy thing to do with shop-teeth, Wincy

thought, smiling to herself as she watched her father lunge toward the apple again. He was laughing so hard that he couldn't have bitten into it, anyhow.

Yes, Wincy thought, she would surely be able to set things to rights in England. After all, she said to herself, as she ducked into the icy water and came up with an apple in her teeth, I've had heaps of experience.

THE END